A DANGEROUS DELIVERY

"You cain't read? Ain't _____ _____. I'll let ya know what the sign said. Git your _____

Slocum halted and _____ _____ it homed in on the road to his left. Huge piles of drossy rock hid all but the shotgun barrel pointed right at him.

"Don't mean no harm. You Calvin Bennigan?"

"You know I am. You got the look of trouble 'bout ya. Git! If you don't, I'll shoot! I'm warnin' ya!"

"Got a letter for you." Slocum carefully pulled it out and held it over his head. He didn't even hear the hammers cocking on the shotgun . . .

DON'T MISS THESE
ALL-ACTION WESTERN SERIES
FROM THE BERKLEY PUBLISHING GROUP

THE GUNSMITH by J. R. Roberts
Clint Adams was a legend among lawmen, outlaws, and ladies. They called him . . . the Gunsmith.

LONGARM by Tabor Evans
The popular long-running series about Deputy U.S. Marshal Custis Long—his life, his loves, his fight for justice.

SLOCUM by Jake Logan
Today's longest-running action Western. John Slocum rides a deadly trail of hot blood and cold steel.

BUSHWHACKERS by B. J. Lanagan
An action-packed series by the creators of Longarm! The rousing adventures of the most brutal gang of cutthroats ever assembled—Quantrill's Raiders.

DIAMONDBACK by Guy Brewer
Dex Yancey is Diamondback, a Southern gentleman turned con man when his brother cheats him out of the family fortune. Ladies love him. Gamblers hate him. But nobody pulls one over on Dex . . .

WILDGUN by Jack Hanson
The blazing adventures of mountain man Will Barlow—from the creators of Longarm!

TEXAS TRACKER by Tom Calhoun
J. T. Law: the most relentless—and dangerous—manhunter in all Texas. Where sheriffs and posses fail, he's the best man to bring in the most vicious outlaws—for a price.

JAKE LOGAN

SLOCUM
AND THE
SCHOOLMARM

J

JOVE BOOKS, NEW YORK

THE BERKLEY PUBLISHING GROUP
Published by the Penguin Group
Penguin Group (USA) Inc.
375 Hudson Street, New York, New York 10014, USA
Penguin Group (Canada), 90 Eglinton Avenue East, Suite 700, Toronto, Ontario M4P 2Y3, Canada
(a division of Pearson Penguin Canada Inc.)
Penguin Books Ltd., 80 Strand, London WC2R 0RL, England
Penguin Group Ireland, 25 St. Stephen's Green, Dublin 2, Ireland (a division of Penguin Books Ltd.)
Penguin Group (Australia), 250 Camberwell Road, Camberwell, Victoria 3124, Australia
(a division of Pearson Australia Group Pty. Ltd.)
Penguin Books India Pvt. Ltd., 11 Community Centre, Panchsheel Park, New Delhi—110 017, India
Penguin Group (NZ), 67 Apollo Drive, Rosedale, North Shore 0632, New Zealand
(a division of Pearson New Zealand Ltd.)
Penguin Books (South Africa) (Pty.) Ltd., 24 Sturdee Avenue, Rosebank, Johannesburg 2196,
South Africa

Penguin Books Ltd., Registered Offices: 80 Strand, London WC2R 0RL, England

SLOCUM AND THE SCHOOLMARM

A Jove Book / published by arrangement with the author

PRINTING HISTORY
Jove edition / February 2008

Copyright © 2008 by The Berkley Publishing Group.
Cover illustration by Sergio Giovine.

ISBN: 978-0-515-14403-1

JOVE®
Jove Books are published by The Berkley Publishing Group,
a division of Penguin Group (USA) Inc.,
375 Hudson Street, New York, New York 10014.
JOVE is a registered trademark of Penguin Group (USA) Inc.
The "J" design is a trademark belonging to Penguin Group (USA) Inc.

PRINTED IN THE UNITED STATES OF AMERICA

10 9 8 7 6 5 4 3 2 1

1

If the town of Dry Water had been any quieter, John Slocum would have thought everyone had died. In his day, he had seen more than a fair number of ghost towns. Dry Water was only slumbering in the afternoon heat, not dead, and whatever ghosts wandered these streets were crowded out on occasion by the living. As he rode down the main street, he looked from left to right and back, noting a man sleeping in the shade afforded by the town bakery. Slocum knew him. He was Jackson Kinney, the former owner of a saloon who had drunk up all his profits and found himself out on the street begging for a nickel to buy yet another glass of beer. Slocum had stood Old Jack for more than a beer to hear his wild stories and skewed outlook on life.

A bit farther down the street the owner of the general store listlessly swept dirt from the floor inside his establishment. Slocum had never seen the man move faster than this slow-as-molasses pace, even when some kids had set fire to his outhouse in back of the store. The man kept to himself, never said more than he had to and left folks alone. Slocum appreciated that, especially when he had to buy supplies. Some store owners could talk a man's ear off.

As he rode past the town's lone remaining saloon, he saw

it, too, was enjoying a brief siesta from the crowd that had bellied up to the bar the night before and would be back again tonight to drown sorrow and kill pain with a few more—or more than a few—shots of whiskey. The proprietor of the Desert Oasis Drinking Emporium and Billiards Hall was a friendly galoot named Alton, and Slocum liked him almost as much as he did Jackson Kinney.

It was quiet all right. Quiet as a cemetery after a burial, but nobody had died.

Slocum liked it this way. Too much of his life recently had been filled with sudden gunfire and thundering stampedes. He had spent the last month on the trail, working to get a herd of balky steers from Texas to the railroad in Abilene, Kansas. Along the way, there had been a never-ending string of rustlers to deal with. What wasn't stolen from the herd had been stricken with some bad disease that killed off damned near a quarter of the beeves. Slocum had been happy to see even a cow town like Abilene. After being paid for his hard work, he had hopped the train and come West. Far West—all the way to California for no reason other than because he had not seen the Pacific Ocean in a spell. Somehow, he had run out of money over at the depot in Pemberton and had somehow drifted to the town of Dry Water, perched right at the northwestern edge of the Mojave Desert, and had never made it all the way to the coast. Life was like that.

Life was also pretty good. Dry Water was a good ways from the railroad station, but that had not killed it the way such distance had so many other small towns. He had found himself thrown off the train, standing on the depot platform and wondering what he would do when a whipcord-thin man had come over to him and given him a job delivering papers. That was all. Slocum had not been asked to shoot anyone or even protect the pouches of legal documents he carried for Judge K. Thomas Tunstell. Just deliver them in a timely fashion. The judge had given him a horse and a dollar a day, and he often succeeded in cadging free meals along the route he rode. Being a legal courier was not what Slocum wanted to do for the rest of his life, but for the moment it allowed him to put a silver dollar or two away toward the day he drifted on. The ocean still beckoned.

But resting up in the quiet town was more than enough for his nerves right now.

The bullet caught the brim of his Stetson and sent it flying into the air. The next bullet cut his horse out from under him, spilling him to the dusty street. As quick as he was, Slocum was caught by surprise and could not get his feet free of his stirrups. The horse toppled over, trapping his leg between dead carcass and ground that had been sunbaked harder than rock.

"Stay down, get down!" Slocum shouted as he fought to get his leg out from under the dead horse. He waved frantically as a drunken Jackson Kinney stumbled out into the street to see what the ruckus was.

"I'll hep ya, Slocum," the man said. Old Jack waved his arms around like a broken windmill and left the safety of the alley.

"Get down!"

Slocum's warning came too late to save the man. Kinney took one more step before a slug caught him in the throat. Slocum saw blood showering down behind Kinney. Then the man's head flopped about as he fell. The shot had torn through his neck and nearly ripped his head off.

Fighting now to get his Colt Navy drawn, Slocum found he could not reach it. He carried it in a cross-draw holster to make drawing easier when he was on horseback. Now it was pinned under his body by the weight of the horse.

Slocum reared up, grabbed and pulled his Winchester from its scabbard. He crashed back down onto the street as he levered a cartridge into the chamber. The bulk of the horse protected him from more gunfire, but it also prevented him from swinging his rifle around and taking care of the swine who had cut down Old Jack Kinney.

More gunfire echoed through the otherwise silent town. Slocum could not see the gunmen but heard the pistols firing.

He tried to sort out the different sounds to guess how many were involved in the gunfight. He stopped at three. Maybe four. More than he could do anything about while trapped under his horse. Using the stock of his rifle, he pried up some of the horse's deadweight off his leg. Wiggling and squirming like a worm, he finally got free. When he tried to stand, his leg gave way under him.

This saved Slocum catching some of the lead death that had already claimed Kinney's life. The gunfire had died down. Now it started again, reminding him of more than one battle during the war.

Slocum flopped on his belly and used the horse as a rest for his rifle. Peering down the barrel, he hunted for a target. He had been a sniper, and a good one, during the war. He usually hit what he aimed at, but first he had to have a target he recognized. People moved around the front of the bank next to the courthouse. Most were probably just coming to see what the fuss was about. Shooting any of them would be akin to murder.

The sound of a horse galloping off should have signaled the end of the fight. It didn't. Slocum caught a glimpse of a blue-and-white checkered shirt and then the flash of the town marshal's badge as he moved toward the front of the bank. Marshal Delgado advanced on the bank, firing steadily. Slocum rolled out from behind his horse to get a better view of the fight. Dragging his leg behind him, he advanced in time to see the marshal empty his six-shooter into a masked man standing in the doorway of the bank. The robber fell to the ground, dead. But another bolted from behind and made a wild dash for the side of the bank.

Slocum wobbled on his gimpy leg but was steady enough to squeeze off a shot. He staggered just a tad at the last instant, causing his round to go downward. But from the way the bank robber went ass over teakettle, it might as well have been a killing shot.

"Freeze," shouted Delgado. "Move and I'll plug you. I swear I will!"

The marshal advanced on the prone robber, six-gun in a

shaking hand. Slocum knew the reason. It wasn't that the marshal was a coward or that the sudden gunfight had unnerved him. He was bluffing. His six-shooter was empty.

The robber tried to get to his feet, but Slocum put a slug into the ground at the man's side.

"You heard him. Don't move!" Slocum shouted. He hobbled forward, brandishing his rifle so the outlaw could see it. If the robber had tried to move a muscle, Slocum would have shot him down.

Delgado went to the bank robber's side and kicked the gun from his hand. Slocum saw the sweat shining on the lawman's broad forehead. Delgado's hair was almost gone on top, but a fuzzy band around the sides almost covered his ears. He was in need of a haircut, but on what Dry Water paid him, doing more than buying a meal a day was out of the question.

Slocum limped up and kept to one side so he could shoot, if necessary. It wasn't. The robber was woozy from his fall. Slocum saw that his slug had ripped off the man's boot heel, tripping him up and sending him to the ground. The unexpected collision with the rock-hard ground had taken all the fight out of him.

"Let's see who's behind that mask," the marshal said, yanking the bandanna from the man's face. He studied the robber a minute and shook his head. "I don't recognize him. How about you, Slocum?"

"Never laid eyes on him, Marshal." Slocum warily came around to get a better look at the man's face. There was a better than decent chance that Slocum might know the bank robber. In his day he had ridden on the other side of the law as much as he had put in an honest day's work. For all the gangs of road agents he had ridden with, this gent was a stranger.

"Come on, you. On your feet." Delgado grabbed the outlaw's fallen pistol, checked to be sure it still had a couple rounds in it, then shoved his own empty six-shooter into his holster.

"You need any help, Marshal?" The timorous call came from inside the bank.

"Nothing you can do, Mr. Williams."

"Who's going to get this . . . this dead man out of my bank lobby?" The banker stared at the other robber that Delgado had stopped. That one had three bullet holes in his chest and wasn't moving.

"Reckon you can get the doc to pick up the body. Or the undertaker. Digger O'Dell's most likely the best choice."

"I'm not paying for this . . . this thief's funeral!" Williams was outraged at the notion. "He tried to rob me and would have, no thanks to you!"

"What do you mean?" Slocum leaned heavily against the wall of the bank building and let the cool brick soak up some of the hurt from his left leg. "If the marshal hadn't been Johnny-on-the-spot, those owlhoots would have gotten away scot-free."

"What were masked men doing riding the streets without being challenged?"

"That's crazy," Slocum said. "They probably pulled up their masks just before going into the bank. And if not, who's to say they hadn't been on the trail and wanted to keep the dust from their noses?"

"Somebody's got to get this body out of here," Williams insisted. The portly banker spun in a full circle, as if looking for someone to browbeat into removing the body. He saw that Slocum wasn't inclined and that Marshal Delgado was already shoving his prisoner down the street toward the jailhouse. "Somebody is responsible!"

"Looks like you are," Slocum said. "Unless you want your customers to step over the body. In this heat, it'll start getting mighty ripe in a few minutes."

Hobbling but feeling the circulation returning to his leg, Slocum headed for the courthouse. Behind him Williams continued his tirade about the city "doing something."

As he reached the steps leading up to the elegant lobby of the courthouse Judge Tunstell had built just for himself, Slocum heard the marshal shouting at him.

"Slocum, wait a minute. Slocum!"

"What is it, Marshal?" Slocum leaned against a white-washed pillar for support. His leg was feeling better, but he didn't want to put his full weight on it until it felt a mite closer to normal. He cradled his rifle in the crook of his left arm as he waited for the lawman to walk across the street.

"You see him, Slocum?"

"Who do you mean?"

"The robber that rode off," Delgado said.

"Heard him. I was pinned under my horse. The lead must have been flying there for a minute or two."

"We got to get after him. I'm not lettin' any low-down *pendejo* come into my town and rob the bank."

"A noble sentiment, Marshal," Slocum said. "You'd better stop jawing and get to riding. He must have gone east, since I was on the west end of town and nobody rode past me."

"You're hereby deputized," Delgado said unexpectedly. "Now come on or I'll toss you in the cell next to the robber."

"As much as I'd like to, Marshal—"

"That leg's fine. You walked this far on it. Besides, you'll be ridin', not walkin' on it."

"Not the leg," Slocum said. "I don't have a horse. Mine was killed." He stared at the dark lump of unmoving horse-flesh in the middle of the street. It was the marshal's job to dispose of dead animals, but Delgado had hardly had a moment for such work after the bank had been held up.

"Then you'll have all the more reason to catch the robber before he gets much farther."

"I can't track him on foot. Besides, it was the judge's horse. He was only loaning it to me for my job."

"I've got a spare. Get your gear on Conchita and let's ride."

"Conchita? You've got to be kidding," Slocum said. The horse was swaybacked and cross-eyed, although he had never looked at it closely enough to tell for sure. Mostly, he had only shaken his head in dismay that anyone paid to feed such a broke-down horse.

"She'll give you the ride of your life. Time's a'wastin'. Move it!"

Slocum looked into the courthouse and knew delivering the judge's papers would have to wait. Grumbling, he returned to where his horse lay drawing flies in the middle of the street. People milled around now, whispering among themselves. Slocum was too pissed off to bother talking to any of them. He got his saddle free from the horse and slung it over his shoulder. The weight staggered him a little, but having the extra load got the kinks out of his bruised and battered leg.

Marshal Delgado waited impatiently in front of the jail. Slocum eyed Conchita with some distrust, but he slung his saddle on her without any protest. He mounted and felt the horse's steady gait.

"But can she do more than walk?" Slocum asked. He was talking to Delgado's back. The marshal had already put the spurs to his own horse and was galloping away in a cloud of dust. "Here goes nothing," Slocum said. When he kicked at Conchita's flanks, the horse took off like a rocket.

Conchita was surprisingly even in gait, and Slocum found himself falling into the peculiar rhythm of riding a new horse. She wasn't fast enough to overtake Delgado, but she didn't have to. The lawman had stopped at the branch of the road. One angled off toward the upper edges of the Mojave and the other went almost due west.

"Which way?" the marshal demanded. "He rode one of these trails. Which one?"

Slocum dropped to the ground and spent ten minutes searching the ground for hoofprints. He scratched his head and only then did he realize he had not picked up his Stetson from where it lay in the Dry Water street. The marshal might want the outlaw for robbing the bank, but Slocum was getting a more personal distaste for the varmint. Horse and hat. He'd have to pay for both of them before they stretched his neck.

Then there was the matter of Old Jack being gunned down.

"Best I can tell on such dry ground—that way." Slocum pointed in the direction of the burning hot desert. In less than a mile the road wound through a rocky patch. The low hills there overlooked a section of hellish land, but Slocum doubted the robber had actually gone into the desert. He probably had a camp near a spring right at the edge of the alkali inferno.

"That might be. Are you sure?"

"Can't say I'd bet the farm on it," Slocum admitted. "If I spotted a dust cloud on the horizon, I'd feel a mite more comfortable."

"Nobody's comfortable in this heat," Delgado said, swiping at his broad face with his bandanna. He glanced over his shoulder down the other branch. "I'm a fair tracker. I see what you do, maybe a tad less, but that was a good choice."

"We're going back to town?" Slocum tried to keep from sounding too hopeful. He didn't cotton much to being deputized like this. More often than not, he had been on the wrong side of the law and this felt wrong. Other than losing his horse—and having a hole put in his hat—he had no quarrel with the outlaw.

Then he remembered how Jackson Kinney had been cut down. Slocum mulled over the man's death a moment and decided the marshal was the best man to handle that murder. He and Kinney had been friends, if the sponger really had any friends in Dry Water. Still, Slocum had taken a liking to him in the weeks he had known him.

"I might need a posse if he headed into that hellhole," the marshal said, staring into the foothills around the edge of the desert. "Hard to find water, even harder to get out alive."

Slocum mounted and trotted alongside the marshal, who turned back toward town. The lawman muttered to himself and made no effort to carry on a conversation with Slocum. That was fine since Slocum was not in a mood for small talk. He still had to deliver the packet of legal papers to the judge, and his entire day had been ruined having his horse shot out from under him. As he rode, he found himself thinking more about the swaybacked nag moving gently beneath him. Conchita had proved herself to be a sturdy, steady mount.

"Leave the horse around back," Delgado said as they drew rein in front of the jailhouse. The words were hardly out of his mouth when a shot rang out. Slocum and Delgado exchanged puzzled looks. The marshal swung in the saddle and tried to find the source of the gunfire. The few people stirring in Dry Water were gathered in front of the bank.

"Might be another robbery," Slocum suggested.

"They're not actin' like it," Delgado said as he shielded his eyes from the setting sun. "I don't like this. I don't like this one little bit." The marshal dropped heavily to the ground and drew his six-gun before going into the jailhouse. Slocum knew the town didn't have a regular deputy to back Delgado up. He heaved a sigh and dismounted. The marshal hadn't told him he was no longer deputized.

Slocum followed the marshal into the office, hand resting on his own six-shooter. The lawman was already working to unlock the door to the small cell block in the rear. As he opened the door, Slocum got a quick view of four cells—and what was in one of them.

"He's dead," Marshal Delgado said as he unlocked the cell door. "Somebody shot the son of a bitch through the window!"

2

Slocum backed from the cell block and went to the door leading to the street. He looked around for a rider leaving town in a hurry. Not even the crowd in front of the bank was moving all that much. Stride long and gun drawn, Slocum rounded the jailhouse and went to the rear where the open windows afforded ventilation—and the chance for someone to kill the prisoner. Dropping to his knees, Slocum caught the setting sun so that it cast long shadows at a low angle across the ground.

"What do you see?"

Slocum looked up. In his concentration he had not heard the marshal come around.

"Squat," Slocum said. "I don't have squat. There's a bunch of dirt kicked around but nothing that means squat."

"So he rode up, poked his gun through the bars and killed the prisoner?"

"Looks like," Slocum said. "Where was the robber shot?"

"In the chest."

"So he was facing the window. Could be he knew who shot him. Might have been the third robber. He could have circled around and come back to town."

11

"Why kill his partner? Nobody was here. He could have broken him out. There wasn't any cause to shoot him."

"No reason we know," Slocum said. He walked around a bit but saw nothing that would help identify the killer. "Might be they had a falling-out. Might be the bank robber on the outside wanted all the money."

"So why kill his partner? Let him rot. He was going to swing for killing Old Jack Kinney. If he had made off with much money, he could have kept riding and never looked back."

"How much did they take?"

Delgado's eyebrows shot up.

"I never got around to asking the banker, not that Roger Williams would give me a straight answer about anything. I swear, that man's tongue ties itself in knots at the mere thought of a simple answer."

"How about a truthful one?"

Delgado looked hard at Slocum but did not reply. He swung around and headed for the bank. Slocum had no cause to follow, but he did. As he stepped out in the street, he saw the banker arguing with the mayor, Claude Grierson. Slocum was too far away to tell what was being said, but neither man looked the least bit pleased. Grierson gestured wildly, poking his finger down the street, then trying to drill a hole through the banker's chest. For his part, Williams did not back off. He truculently thrust his face until it was only inches from the mayor's. Even at this distance, Slocum could see how livid the banker was. His face was a fiery red, and his hands shook as he balled them into tight fists. Slocum wondered if he would end up in court, testifying how the town banker punched the mayor.

The mayor shoved Williams back against the wall. All Slocum heard Grierson say was, "That goddamn miner."

Before Williams could respond, Delgado's approach quelled whatever argument raged between the two men. Grierson muttered something only the banker could hear, swung around and stalked off. Slocum picked up the pace and got closer in time to hear Williams answering the marshal's questions.

"... haven't counted it all yet, Marshal. But it's a princely sum. Might be as much as ten thousand dollars they made off with. I want it back! I ... I'll give a fifty-dollar reward for bringing the crooks to justice."

"Now that's real generous of you, Mr. Williams," the marshal said. Slocum heard the contempt in the lawman's voice. He had to wonder what idiot would offer fifty dollars to recover ten thousand.

"I'll double it if the robbers are put on trial, too. No, no, make that double if they are *convicted*. No reason to pass out money if they're on trial and squirm off the hook. I know these people in Dry Water. They'd like to see a bandit stick it to me. They're too dumb to realize it was their money the robbers took."

"I'll let folks know," Delgado said.

"How come you had so much money on hand?" Slocum asked.

Williams's mouth moved like a fish washed up on the bank. Then the bank president got his wits about him.

"This is a transfer point for a lot of money, Slocum. Sometimes I hold more than usual. This was one of those times."

"So the robbers were either lucky or knew you had a pile of greenbacks in your vault," Slocum said. "Which might it be? Lucky or smart?"

"You work for the judge," Williams said. "It's not proper for me to say another word to you. When the marshal catches the robbers, you might have to help the judge, and it wouldn't be right to look like they were being railroaded."

"No, reckon not," Slocum allowed. He read more than this in the banker's now glib response to the question. Williams really managed to avoid answering at all.

"I've got work to do, Slocum," Delgado said. "Run on about your business. Thanks for your help."

"It's nothing, Marshal." And as far as Slocum was concerned, that was all it amounted to. He had tracked, ridden and drawn his gun, but all he had to show for it was a dead horse. And a hole in the brim of his hat. Remembering the Stetson, Slocum went back to where his horse lay on its side, drawing flies and the more aggressive of the town's hungry dogs. He found his hat in the dust, brushed off what he could and then settled it back on his head. The sun had set, but it would rise again in the morning and Slocum would need the hat brim to shield his eyes as he got the hell out of Dry Water. What peacefulness there was had disappeared with the first gunshot.

He had no idea how long it would be until the marshal found someone to blame for the murder in his very own jail, but it would happen. It had to or the lawman would find himself replaced. Being marshal of Dry Water probably paid less than twenty dollars in scrip a month, but Delgado had a place to sleep and the work was easy. Or it had been until today.

Slocum brushed dust off the leather pouch he carried the judge's papers in, then tramped down the street for the courthouse. It might be too late for the judge to be in his office, but Slocum wanted to deliver the papers so he could go find that vast expanse of Pacific Ocean with its endless beaches and not a single steer in view.

Inside the courthouse he heard small sounds echoing from the direction of the judge's office. Slocum rapped twice on the closed door. From inside came the sound of papers being shoved into drawers and those drawers closing, then, "Come on in."

"Evening, Judge," Slocum greeted. "Got the papers."

"My God, man, after all that's happened today, you still brought me my paltry papers? Sit down, Mr. Slocum. Take a load off those feet."

Slocum dropped the pouch with the legal documents on the judge's desk and then sat carefully in the leather chair. It was so comfortable Slocum felt that he might just drift off to sleep. With Judge Tunstell that would be a mistake. Not only was the man razor-sharp, he might well pick Slocum's pocket.

Slocum had seen how Judge K. Thomas Tunstell ran the town with an iron fist. His orders all went through the mayor and marshal, but they were his and his alone. The man perched like a hungry captor on the edge of his chair, keen eyes fixed on Slocum. Tunstell cleared his throat. Slocum was fascinated watching the man's Adam's apple bounce up and down in his scrawny neck. Skeletal fingers formed a tent under the man's close-shaven chin as his brows furrowed in careful thought.

"Would you like a drink? How silly of me. Of course you would. Tell me all about your chase, Mr. Slocum. Was there any hope of finding the man who escaped?"

"Not much," Slocum said. He took the crystal glass with three fingers of whiskey he knew was better than anything Alton over at the Desert Oasis was ever likely to pour and stared into the swirling surface. Then he sipped at it.

"Ah, you appreciate fine Tennessee sipping whiskey," Tunstell said. "You are more than you appear, Mr. Slocum."

"No, sir, I'm not. I'm exactly what you see."

"Perhaps my vision is a bit sharper than others."

"Your horse is still out in the middle of the street. One of the bank robbers shot it out from under me just before Jackson Kinney got gunned down."

"I know all about that. Tell me about the pursuit and . . . the aftermath." Tunstell peered hard at Slocum, as if he could nail him to the chair with his gaze. Slocum knew such tactics worked well in court. The one trial he had watched Tunstell preside over, the judge had used just such a look to keep a lid on both attorneys and their wild-ass notions of what constituted the law. In K. Thomas Tunstell's court, *his* word was the law.

"Lost the trail where the road branches. The robber might have ridden into the malpais—"

"The badlands?"

"The badlands," Slocum continued, "and then again, he might have gone on toward Pemberton or cut across to Barstow. By now he could be all the way to Sacramento."

"I think not, Mr. Slocum. But then, neither do you. That was an exaggeration simply to show that the robber would not have been foolish enough to return to kill his partner. What do you think of that?"

"Don't know what to make of it," Slocum said. "If I'd got clean away with as much money as the banker claims, I wouldn't stop running until I reached Oregon."

"How much did Mr. Williams claim was taken? I have not heard."

"He was throwing around a number so big it made my head ache," Slocum said. "Ten thousand."

"So much?" Tunstell's eyebrows arched and wiggled like furry caterpillars on a hot griddle. Slocum wondered at the consternation the judge showed.

"That's about what Marshal Delgado said. Seems a great pile of money to be keeping at a bank in Dry Water."

"Indeed," Tunstell said. He sipped at his whiskey, then said, "I've got another job for you."

"Think it's time for me to move on."

"You need to work off the price of the horse I loaned you. That was a mighty fine mare."

"Gelding," Slocum said. "The horse you gave me was a gelding."

"Was it? I have so many, it's hard to keep track of them all." Tunstell sipped a bit more on his whiskey, watching Slocum closely.

"That is a mighty fine stallion. The big black one," Slocum said. He knew it was Tunstell's pride and joy. The judge rode around on that horse like he was king of the world. As far as the citizens of Dry Water went, that was not far from the truth. Slocum wondered how the judge might try to stop him if he really took it into his head to leave.

"I'll pay you twice what I was," the judge said. "And forget about you having to repay me for the dead horse."

"But I'd have to buy a new horse," Slocum said. "Delivering legal documents for you on foot would get to be a real chore."

"I wouldn't want to think you were shirking your duty, Mr. Slocum," Tunstell said. "I will loan you another horse. No, not mine," he added, more sharply. The judge opened his desk drawer and took out an envelope. He made a big deal of opening it and studying the contents. Tunstell took out a steel-nibbed pen, dipped it in the inkwell at his right hand, then signed the last page with a flourish. He blotted his signature, tucked the pages back into the envelope and handed it to Slocum. "Deliver this."

Slocum saw a man's name neatly printed on the envelope.

"Don't know him. Where do I find him?"

"Go south of town about five miles until you see a sign directing you to the Holey Mine."

"Just hand the papers over?"

"Nothing more. I need it done quickly."

"Mighty late. Should I ride all night?"

"First thing in the morning be on the road, Mr. Slocum. I expect an answer back by sundown tomorrow."

Slocum stared at the envelope he held, then damned himself as he tucked it away in his coat pocket. He should be on his way. He could buy Conchita from the marshal for what few dollars he had saved working for the judge. Somehow, although Slocum was never one to shy away from trouble, he did not want to lock horns with Judge Tunstell right now. The man's manner brooked no challenge. Moreover, it had been a hell of a day and Slocum wanted nothing more than to grab a good meal and then curl up in his bed and sleep till the sun was over the mountains to the east.

He finished his whiskey and left without another word. He thought Tunstell made a satisfied noise but did not bother turning to see. It was enough that he had given in to the man's demands. For a while.

3

It was cold as only a desert can chill the bones. Slocum rode along before sunrise, found the road south and was a mile toward the turnoff when the sun finally poked its fiery eye above the low hills. The chill he had felt quickly disappeared and was replaced by the promise of a blast furnace day. He pulled down the brim of his hat to keep the light from his eyes. Judge Tunstell's horse under him was a sturdy gelding, making him think that the judge knew every detail of every horse he owned. Tunstell had been toying with him like a cat plays with a field mouse when talking about the dead horse.

Slocum tried to figure out the judge. The man was content being a big frog in a small puddle, and that didn't make a whole lot of sense. Tunstell was nothing if not a politician and had designs on something more. Or he should have. Slocum could not be sure what was behind Tunstell's actions. He ran Dry Water as surely as if he had a gun to everyone's head, but it was a benevolent dictatorship. The entire time he had been in town, Slocum had not heard a bad word spoken about the judge. The banker was another matter, but that was hardly unusual.

He didn't put it beyond Roger Williams to lie about the money stolen from the bank. All the banker had to do was salt away what remained and call it missing, too. The depositors would be out their money and someone else would take the blame. But why had he claimed so much had been taken? Ten thousand dollars was a princely sum that had no reason being stuffed into a vault inside the First Bank of Dry Water.

The sun rose enough to cause sweat to bead on Slocum's leathery face. He turned eastward to the hills where the sign pointed toward the Holey Mine. Whether the miner had a curious sense of humor or was mostly illiterate, Slocum didn't know or much care. He had a letter to deliver before he could return to town. Some whiskey would settle the dust in his mouth, even if the pop skull Alton dished out wasn't anywhere near as good as the judge's whiskey.

The judge had said it was five miles to the turnoff but had said nothing about the distance to the mine. Slocum had gone more than five miles eastward when he spotted a watering hole. He only had to relax his grip on the reins for the horse to veer from the road and head straight for the pond. It always amazed him how watering holes appeared out of nowhere in the desert. He was close enough to rocky foothills for some water to run off and fill the pond, but he saw no obvious arroyos leading into the pond. That meant it was fed from underground springs.

"Whoa, wait a minute," Slocum said, drawing back hard on the reins as his horse tried to gallop to the water. From horseback he looked around the pond for any sign of bones. Alkali water might look all right and smell fine to a horse, but once in an animal's belly it killed in a short time. He saw no trace that the water might be bad.

Slocum dismounted and held his horse back as he knelt to sample the water.

"Sweet," Slocum said, releasing his hold on the reins. The horse began gulping down gallons of water. Slocum took off his hat and filled with water, dumping it over his head to cool himself off. Then he drank some more, filled his canteen and finally dragged his horse away. He didn't want the horse bloating on him almost ten miles from town. That was a long walk back that neither of them would appreciate.

As he went to mount, he saw a hoofprint in the mud on the far side of the pond. He circled and looked at it. Fresh tracks. From the look of it, the rider had come out of the hills, then reversed course and returned. Standing in his stirrups, Slocum looked hard for the rider.

Seeing nothing, he put his heels to his horse's flanks and got back on the road. He had hardly gone a mile when the flash of sunlight off bright metal caught his attention. He turned a mite in the saddle and saw a rider along a distant ridge, heading northward. Slocum reached back and got his field glasses from his saddlebags and focused on the rider. He caught his breath. While a shirt that carried such a blue-and-white-checked pattern was common, the last time he had seen it was on the bank robber who had escaped.

Slocum followed the solitary figure for a couple minutes, then the rider disappeared over the ridge, following a trail down the far side. Out of Slocum's line of sight, the man could be headed anywhere. After putting his field glasses back, he considered whether to track the man. He shrugged it off. The rider might have been the robber, but that meant less to Slocum than delivering the judge's letter. More than his need to fulfill his duty, Slocum might have been chasing a will-o'-the-wisp. The rider could be anybody. The shirt was store-bought, and half the men roaming these hills might have identical ones. That the man had been in a powerful hurry and had probably watered his horse at the same watering hole meant nothing.

Duty first. Then if Slocum happened to spot the man again, he could satisfy his curiosity. As much as he hated to admit it, the fifty dollars the banker had offered for catching the robbers was mighty appealing to Slocum.

A slow smile came to his lips. If he happened on the robber's camp and came across the ten thousand dollars Williams claimed had been stolen, fifty dollars would seem paltry. Slocum was not above stealing from a crook and keeping the

money. That much, even in greenbacks, would take him a
powerful long way from Dry Water. To the Pacific and up the
coast to Oregon. He would still have more than enough left
to buy himself a string of Appaloosas and do a little breeding somewhere around the Dalles.

When he found where the rider had crossed the road on
his way into the foothills, Slocum almost followed. The lure
of all that money was just about more than he could over-
come. But the sun beat down on his body, causing him to
sweat like a pig. And the sweatiest spot was under the letter
he was supposed to deliver for Judge Tunstell. Before it became totally sweat-soaked and unreadable, he had to find the
recipient and hand it over.

Slocum ignored the hoofprints leading into the hills and
kept on riding. Within three miles he found a trail to the
Holey Mine. From the condition of the trail, it seemed there
was not much ore left as damned little in way of supplies
had been taken up. Weeds grew in the twin ruts and even a
cactus had begun slipping its thorn-covered pads into the
roadway. Nobody traveled this way much.

Still, the evidence of mining activity grew as Slocum
turned up the steep hill. On either side he saw tailings puk-
ing forth like black bile from the hillside. The fact that these
mines were deserted told Slocum there wasn't much gold to
be found around here. That still hadn't stopped Calvin Bennigan from putting up a gate across the road with a NO TRES-
PASSING sign on it. The only problem with the gate was that
there was no fence on either side. Slocum rode around.

He pulled the soggy letter from his pocket and matched
the name to a sign on a weathered post. Satisfied he was on
the right trail, he kept riding.

"You cain't read? Ain't no disgrace, so I'll let ya know
what the sign said. Git your cracker ass off my property!"

Slocum halted and looked around. He saw no one, but
homed in on the road to his left. Huge piles of drossy rock
hid all but the shotgun barrel pointed right at him.

"Don't mean no harm. You Calvin Bennigan?"

"You know I am. You got the look of trouble 'bout ya. Git! If you don't, I'll shoot! I'm warnin' ya!"

"Got a letter for you." Slocum carefully pulled it out and held it over his head. He didn't even hear the hammers cocking on the shotgun. Bennigan must have already cocked the weapon. Sensing what was going to happen, Slocum flung himself off the horse and hit the ground hard as heavy lead shot tore past. He landed hard and pushed himself up to his hands and knees. The shotgun had spun off a ways and pointed toward the sky.

It took him a second to realize what was going on. The miner had not been behind the shotgun. He had rigged it up with string around the trigger so he could pull it and discharge the weapon from elsewhere. The shotgun had only been held in place by heavy rocks on either side of the barrel and probably a large one immediately behind the stock to take up the recoil when it was fired. It was a trap and a clever one. Slocum had been too preoccupied with the shotgun barrel to take note that the voice had come from the other side of the trail.

"Don't shoot," Slocum said. In his position on all fours, there was no way he could go for his own six-shooter. He craned his neck around and saw a miner holding a heavy Remington in both hands. The man's hands shook hard and he squinted at Slocum, one eye screwed tightly shut. From the facial tic under the closed eye, Slocum guessed Bennigan was not merely aiming. His eye might be permanently shut from the spasms.

"I outfoxed ya, din't I?"

"That you did," Slocum said. "If you'll take the letter, I'll be on my way."

"Don't want no letter. Don't want nuthin' 'cept for you to skedaddle."

"It's my job to give you the letter. Why don't I just leave it here on the ground for you, get on my horse and ride on back to Dry Water?"

"I kin kill ya where you are."

"Why waste more ammo? You got me," Slocum said. The

trouble was, that summed it up too well. If he moved a muscle for his six-gun, Bennigan could fire a couple times before
he could drag out the Colt, roll, aim and fire. The miner might
not be a good shot but at this range he didn't have to be.

"I set that trap fer cusses like you," Bennigan said. "Don't
want no claim jumpers sneakin' up on me."

"You must have seen me coming from a ways off,"
Slocum said. He shifted his weight off his right hand. Grabbing for the pistol in his cross-draw holster would be dangerous, but the crazy old coot was as likely to shoot him in
the back as talk. Better to go down trying to save himself as
let Bennigan shoot him in the back with a black-powder pistol that had seen its best day ten years earlier.

"Keep a sharp eye out, the one eye that's good," Bennigan
said. The miner moved around to keep directly behind
Slocum. He might be a recluse and suspicious of anybody
coming onto his property, but he was no fool. Staying alive
required him to have some native cunning.

"I—"

"You don't got to do nuthin' but leave. You rear on up onto
your knees and keep them hands of yers where I kin see 'em.
If they ain't grabbin' a piece of sky, you're a dead man."

Slocum did as he was told. The sharp rock cut into his
knees, but he was more intent on the shadow on the ground.
That told him where Bennigan stood. The shaky shadow
showed the miner had not lowered his guard—or his gun.

"What now?"

"You git on that horse the best you kin, usin' only yer
right hand. Keep the left up high. Git on the horse and never
come back here again."

"What's your beef with Judge Tunstell?"

"Ain't got one, 'cept he's a damned crook!"

Slocum heard anger coming into Bennigan's voice and
knew it was time to retreat. Getting himself back-shot for the
judge served no purpose.

"I'm getting to my feet now," Slocum said, keeping his
hands high. He got his horse and clumsily mounted.

"Both hands in the air 'til yer off my property. I'll drill you, I will, if you don't do as I say!"

Slocum had no trouble using his knees to turn his horse and get it walking off Bennigan's claim. He skirted the gate across the road and retraced his path a good hundred yards before lowering his hands. Glancing back, he saw the miner crouched behind a strategically placed mound of mined rock. When he had ridden in, Slocum wondered at the small hills dotting the area on either side of the road. Now he knew they were not carelessly placed. Bennigan could dart from one to the next to hold off any invasion of his property. He had done what he could to fortify the claim.

"What the hell's got that wild hair up your ass?" Slocum muttered. He dragged out the envelope and saw his sweat had caused the glue to come unstuck. He pulled out the sweat-damp sheet and held it up so he could read it. It took only a couple lines for him to realize this was the judge's order to Calvin Bennigan to vacate the property for nonpayment of taxes. Slocum bristled at this. He had returned from the war, his parents and brother dead, to Slocum's Stand in Calhoun, Georgia, intending only to farm and recuperate from serious wounds. A carpetbagger judge had taken a fancy to land that had been ceded to the Slocum family by George II. It would have made a perfect stud farm, but the judge had gone about getting it in the wrong way.

Nonpayment of taxes, the Reconstruction judge had said through his lying teeth. The judge and a hired gunman had ridden out to seize the property from Slocum. Two fresh graves near the springhouse had been their legacy. And a trail of wanted posters for killing a federal judge had been Slocum's.

He folded the sheet and tucked it back into the envelope. He frowned as something else gnawed at the corners of his memory. Miner. Calvin. Calvin Bennigan. The mayor and the banker had been arguing about a miner. Slocum could not be certain but he thought he had heard "Cal" in the midst of their argument immediately after the bank had been robbed. It had struck him as odd that this would be what the two men were fighting about when the bank robbers hadn't been caught.

Slocum swung in the saddle and scanned the terrain high above where Bennigan undoubtedly hid, waiting for Slocum to get the hell off his land. Maybe that rider had been the remaining robber. It certainly wasn't Calvin Bennigan, but maybe Bennigan was hiding the thief. That would explain why Grierson and Williams were talking about the miner so soon after the bank robbery. Did they suspect Bennigan of being in cahoots with the robbers? It was a stretch for Slocum to think Bennigan might be the mastermind behind the robbery, but if so much money had been stolen, as Williams claimed, maybe it was so.

But that almost meant that Williams and Grierson had to know before the robbery that Bennigan was involved. Their argument had come too soon after the robbery for any other explanation. Slocum wondered if Marshal Delgado had a stack of wanted posters with Calvin Bennigan's picture on them.

He rode back along the road, pausing where the rider's hoofprints had gone into the foothills. He shrugged it off. It had been a hell of a day. He had been shot at by an angry miner and sent on his way. That was enough to get him back to Dry Water to report to the judge as quick as a flash.

Slocum was half asleep in the saddle when he reached the outskirts of Dry Water. He shook himself awake and looked down the street at the fine courthouse and at the calaboose, and then made a quick decision. He dropped heavily to the ground and went into the marshal's office. Delgado worked furiously oiling his rifle. Parts were scattered across the desk and he looked up, his dark eyes hot and angry.

"What do you want, Slocum?"

"Pleased to see you, too, Marshal," Slocum said.

"You were out of town all day. I was not," Delgado said. "The mayor has offered to fire me because of the bank robbery and—" Delgado jerked his thumb in the direction of the cells. Slocum knew the dead prisoner weighed heavily on Delgado. "What do you want?"

"Could just be passing the time of day," Slocum said, "or it could be you might tell me something about Calvin Bennigan."

"The miner outside of town?" Delgado shrugged. "Nothing to say about him. He is a hermit. Most miners are. When he comes to town, he does not get drunker than anyone else." He thought for a moment and shook his head. "I have never thrown him into one of my cells." A dark cloud formed on the marshal's face. "A good thing for him. He might have ended up dead, too."

"No wanted posters on him?"

"What is it you are saying?"

Slocum idly leafed through the stack of posters on the edge of Delgado's desk. He saw nothing that implicated Bennigan in a prior robbery.

"Just a thought. I've got to get to the judge's office before he goes home for the night."

"Tunstell never goes home," groused the marshal. He made shooing motions to get Slocum out of his office. Slocum left, stood in the cool evening and felt the sweat on his forehead evaporating. He took out the letter Bennigan had refused and stared at it again. Then he set off for the courthouse.

As before, the place was deserted save for the single light coming from the judge's office. Slocum wondered if the marshal was right about Tunstell never leaving.

"Slocum, that you? I saw you ride into town. Where have you been?"

"Right here, Judge," Slocum said. He dropped the sweat-stained letter onto the desk. Tunstell stared at it for a moment, then looked up into Slocum's green eyes.

"You did not deliver it."

"Couldn't. Almost got my head blown off by a shotgun blast, then shot in the back by that son of a bitch. I showed it to him, but he wouldn't take it."

"He knew what was in the letter," Judge Tunstell said in a flat voice. "That doesn't leave me any choice." He rummaged in his desk drawer and pulled out a thick sheaf of papers. He riffled through them, found the last page and signed with a flourish before handing them to Slocum.

"What am I supposed to do with these?"

"Those are eviction papers, duly signed and approved by the court."

"That's you."

"That's right, Mr. Slocum. Me. Give them to the marshal. It's his job to serve process. I want Cal Bennigan off that claim by the end of the week."

Slocum heard the implied "come hell or high water." What it was about Bennigan's mine that stirred up so much trouble in Dry Water was going to be settled soon. Slocum was sure it would be at the point of a gun. Given how obstinate the miner had seemed, there was likely to be bloodshed.

He was glad he didn't have to be a part of it.

4

Slocum sauntered back toward the marshal's office with the thick wad of papers ordering Calvin Bennigan off his property. In no particular hurry because he remembered too well how he had felt when the carpetbagger judge had come to throw him off the family land, Slocum peered into the Desert Oasis. There were a few men bellied up to the bar, but no serious drinking had started. He licked his lips, thinking how just a taste of whiskey would sit well with him. Then he backed away and turned toward Delgado's office. Duty first. The sooner he passed this unsavory chore along to the lawman, the sooner he could be out of town.

Slocum was not certain when he had decided that Dry Water was no longer a decent stopover for him on his way to the coast. Desert held no real attraction for him. Not like standing on a bluff looking out over a vast expanse of water. But mountains were where he felt most alive. He could ride the Kansas prairie and appreciate the majesty of the open range, but seeing the soaring Grand Tetons or the Front Range looking down over Denver made his heart beat just a tad faster.

"The ocean first, then the mountains," he promised himself out loud. He opened the door to the jailhouse and poked his head in. Louder, he called, "Marshal? Marshal Delgado?"

No response. He looked around the door. The office was empty. Crossing it quickly, he looked into the cell block at the rear of the jailhouse. Also empty.

Slocum grumbled to himself. He had no idea where the lawman had gotten off to. He dropped the eviction papers on the man's desk. Let Delgado find them and serve process when he got around to it. Still, Slocum felt an obligation to tell the lawman that the judge was in a mighty big hurry to get Bennigan off his claim. If Delgado postponed it, he would end up in hot water with both the mayor and the judge. In a town like Dry Water, that would mean he would be hunting for a new job somewhere else entirely before sundown the next day.

Slocum pulled up a chair, rocked it back on its rear legs so he could balance against the wall and sat gingerly. He pulled down his shot-up hat and within minutes was asleep. It had been a long day.

Slocum came awake with a start when the door banged open.

"What the hell are you doing here, Slocum?"

"Waiting for you, Marshal," he said. "Got papers from the judge he wants served right away."

"Damnation." Delgado almost collapsed into his chair. He pawed through the pages and then looked up. "You know what these are, don't you?"

"Kind of hard for me not to. That's the way Judge Tunstell handed them to me."

"You were out at Bennigan's claim to deliver a letter ordering him to quit the claim. When he didn't vamoose, you told the judge." Delgado tapped the tall pile of papers. "You got these."

"That's it in a nutshell," Slocum said. He tipped the chair forward so all four legs were on the floor. Standing, he pushed his hat up. "I've done my duty. Do yours."

"Hold on, Slocum," the marshal called. "Get your ass back here."

Slocum turned and saw Delgado holding a battered

badge. He almost kept from catching it when the lawman tossed it to him.

"Pin that on your chest."

Slocum held the badge as if it had turned fiery hot.

"You're not deputizing me again. I went along before because that owlhoot shot at me. Killed the horse I was riding, shot Old Jack, maybe killed your prisoner. But I'm not letting you deputize me to serve process on a miner whose only crime is not paying his taxes."

"There's more to it than that. You're no man's fool, Slocum. You're going with me. I need someone to watch my back."

Slocum started to say no but saw the iron resolve in Delgado's face. The lines were etched on his forehead as if scored across old copper. His jaw was set and his dark eyes blazed.

Slocum heaved a sigh and nodded.

"I'll do it, but this time only. And I'm not wearing the damn badge." He tucked it into his vest pocket.

"Don't care if you do, but you're coming with me. You're the only one in town who knows what I'll be up against. I don't want to shoot Bennigan if I can get him to leave."

"You won't. He'll only go feet first," Slocum said. The look in the miner's eyes told him that. This was a matter of life or death. There was no ground in between the two extremes.

"With you, I might be able to hog-tie him and drag him away. He won't like it, and I don't, either. But it's the only chance Bennigan has of staying alive."

Slocum knew that was probably true. The pair of them might be able to circle the miner and catch him. Anything less than all the skill Slocum had acquired during long years on the frontier, watching and learning from Indians, hunting and being hunted, fighting for his life, would result in Bennigan's death.

"Dawn?"

"Dawn," Delgado said, relaxing a mite. "You won't try to hightail it, will you?"

"Not my horse. I'd be stealing a horse if I did." Slocum hesitated, then asked, "What are you willing to sell Conchita for?"

"We'll dicker over her when we get back and have Bennigan safely locked up."

"I'll be at the Desert Oasis. Alton owes me a drink or two," Slocum said.

"Be sure he doesn't give you the tarantula juice that causes your eyes to bug out and your belly to shrink like a prune. I want you in good shape tomorrow."

Slocum laughed as he left. The smile on his face died as he walked down the street to the saloon. The only reason he had agreed to go with Delgado was the reason the lawman stated. If the marshal took anyone else, Bennigan was likely to end up dead. Slocum owed the miner nothing but felt a bond with him. He had lost his family's land to an identical legal ploy. Slocum knew nothing of the background but could hardly believe Bennigan was more in arrears on his taxes than a dozen other miners out in the hills. For whatever reason, Judge Tunstell had taken a fancy to the land and this was his way of getting it.

As he stepped onto the wood planking outside the saloon, he heard someone whisper his name. Slocum looked down the boardwalk and saw a shadowy figure at the edge of the building.

"Come here. Come on!" The man gestured for Slocum to join him.

"I'm going to get a drink. Join me or not," Slocum said. "It don't make no never mind to me." As he started to push open the swinging doors, the man moved from the shadows and grabbed for Slocum's arm.

Without thinking, Slocum whirled around, broke the grip and grabbed the man by the lapels. He cocked his other hand back in a fist, ready to punch hard. He hesitated when he saw he had grabbed hold of Roger Williams.

"What do you want?" Slocum asked the banker.

"I mean you no harm, Slocum. Really!"

Slocum relaxed his grip and shoved the banker back a step.

"You got a piss-poor way of showing it."

"I have an offer. A lucrative one. Just for you."

Slocum stood and waited. Williams got nervous and shuffled his feet, then summoned up whatever courage he had and blurted out what he had to say.

"Two hundred dollars. I'll give you two hundred in gold if he never makes it back to town."

"Who? The owlhoot that robbed your bank?"

"No, no, Calvin Bennigan. I don't want him coming back to Dry Water and raising a fuss."

"What do I have to do with this Bennigan?" Slocum fixed his steely gaze on the banker, who tried to stiffen his spine but failed. His eyes darted all over the place like a little boy caught stealing from the apple barrel.

"You're going out with the marshal to evict Bennigan tomorrow. He's a troublemaker. I don't want him to drag this out. He'll put up a fuss. I know him. It won't be hard to just plug him."

"You mean you want me to murder him."

"Call it what you like, Slocum. I don't want him returning to town alive. I'll even pay for the funeral so he won't have to be buried in the potter's field."

"That's right generous of you," Slocum said. "Now I have some serious drinking to do."

Slocum left Williams standing outside. He felt his gut churning. If he had stayed with the banker another second, there would have been need of a new grave to be dug in the cemetery.

Somehow, the whiskey didn't taste near as good as Slocum had anticipated.

The sun wouldn't poke over the distant hills for another half hour. The desert chill settled all the way into Slocum's bones, but he hardly cared. He would be done with this disagreeable chore soon. Delgado had wanted him along to keep Bennigan from getting too rambunctious, but bringing the miner back to Dry Water might be just as dangerous for Bennigan if Williams was up to offering blood money for his death.

When Delgado came around the corner of the jailhouse, he was leading Conchita but sat astride his own horse.

Seeing Slocum's puzzled expression, the marshal said, "Bennigan doesn't have a horse and I'll be damned if I'll put up with that balky mule of his. For all I know, he ate the critter."

Slocum mounted and wondered what he should tell the marshal. Delgado was sharp enough to see his hesitation.

"Spit it out, Slocum. You've got something you want to say. So just come on out and say it."

"Why would Williams want Bennigan dead?"

"What'd he do, go and offer you money to be certain Bennigan ended up dead?"

"Yeah."

"Son of a bitch." Delgado continued to grumble, switching to Spanish and then back to English. "He's poking his nose where it doesn't belong."

"Why? What's so all-fired important about the Holey Mine?"

Delgado shrugged. "Politics. That's all it is. It's Bennigan's bad luck he got caught in the middle." Delgado glared at him. "You try to shoot Bennigan and I'll see a rope around your neck."

"You make it so easy to wear a deputy's badge."

Delgado had to laugh.

They rode out of town and headed south. After taking a break to rest their horses at the watering hole, Slocum saw the day-old tracks he'd noticed before. Delgado saw his interest.

"What are you staring so hard at, Slocum? Those are old tracks."

"Weren't yesterday," Slocum said. "I watched the rider along yonder ridge."

Delgado followed where Slocum pointed. The marshal sat a little straighter in the saddle.

"Who was it? The bank robber?"

"Might have been," Slocum said. "I seem to remember the bank robber wearing a blue-and-white checkerboard shirt like the rider."

"You let him go?" Delgado roared. "There's a huge reward on the man's head and you let him go?"

"What huge reward?" Slocum asked. "The fifty dollars Williams offered? He offered me two hundred to kill Bennigan."

"Fifty? The bank's put up a thousand-dollar reward."

"Seems Williams is mighty generous when it comes to offering money to see people dead."

"I want the robber. He killed my prisoner. Nobody's ever done that to me before. I swear, Slocum, nobody's ever going to do it again!" Delgado began shouting in Spanish so fast Slocum could pick out only a word here and there. Delgado was not happy that the robber had slipped away yesterday.

When the marshal slowed enough for Slocum to get a word in edgewise, he said, "I never saw the robber's face."

"Of course not," Delgado snapped. "He wore a damn mask."

"The man I saw wore the same color shirt. That's mighty slim evidence to go tearing off after a man who might have nothing to do with the robbery."

"You were just too antsy to tell Bennigan to get the hell off his property."

"You think that, Marshal?" Slocum reached to trace the outline of the badge in his pocket. He was within a second of throwing the badge in the lawman's face. He didn't care if he stole the judge's horse or not. He was fed up with Dry Water and the people in it.

"I'm sorry, Slocum. I'm too angry over having that owlhoot killed in my jail to think straight. You don't have any ax to grind."

"I'm just a drifter," Slocum said.

"Don't drift on until we've seen this to its end. Then you can go, with my blessings." Delgado hesitated, then said, "With Conchita. I'll give you the horse if you stay with me on this."

"What do you want me to do?"

Delgado paused, looking from the road to the Holey Mine and then to the ridge where Slocum had seen the rider.

"Go after him. Find out if he's the one who robbed the bank. I'll deal with Bennigan. He's a cranky old turd, but I can get him back to town alive."

"You know he won't think twice about plugging you," Slocum said.

"I'm a lawman. I live with that every day, wondering if some drunk cowboy's going to shoot me in the back because it's Thursday or if a road agent will put me in his sights. I can handle Bennigan just fine."

"I could see to Bennigan with you and then go after the rider," Slocum said.

"Time's a'wasting," Delgado replied. "Every hour might put more miles between us."

"He seems to be sticking close to town," Slocum said, but his mind was already on the trail and how he would track the rider over the rocky terrain. That was a better use of his time and talent than chevying a half-starved miner.

"He might have something keeping him here," Delgado said.

"He might not have killed his partner in your jail. He might want to settle the score with whoever did. The shooting doesn't make any sense at all."

"He might have circled and come back to shoot his partner so the partner wouldn't reveal his identity," Delgado said.

"But nobody was in the jail," Slocum said. "And he got all the money."

They could sit and argue all day and never come to an answer. It struck Slocum that he and Delgado had switched sides in the futile argument. The marshal was now making all the arguments Slocum had done and now Slocum had come around to believe what the marshal originally had thought—that the robber was innocent of shooting his partner. Finding the robber was the only way to discover what had really gone on.

"See you back in town," Slocum said.

"Here's hoping we both have our man," Delgado said.

Slocum set off along the trail taken by the rider. After an hour he reached the ridgeline and found the narrow path cut along it. Here and there he saw small traces of a rider passing recently. He hardly paid such spoor any attention. He was more interested in the spot where the rider had vanished from sight, heading down the back side of the hill.

This was a game trail, but hoofprints were visible as Slocum studied the ground. He looked up and tried to figure where the rider had been going. The steep slope ended in a rocky ravine that worked its way back into the hills. Hot wind blew from that direction, giving Slocum a hint of smoke. He inhaled more deeply and a slow smile came to his lips. Cooking meat. Someone had a camp upwind.

The steep trail forced him to dismount and lead his horse down to the bottom of the ravine. At one time a considerable amount of water had rushed from higher elevations and cut a deep gorge, but how long ago that had been was a mystery. Even the hardy cactus and creosote bushes that somehow survived in the burning desert found it difficult to grow here.

Once in the ravine, Slocum mounted again and rode slowly. Now and then he took a whiff of the air to make sure he was going in the right direction. He tried to determine how far he was from the source of the smoke, but there was no way of telling. The wind whipped through the deep V in the hills. The source of the cooking fire might be a mile or more away in some canyon.

Slocum hesitated before riding deeper into the mountains. He studied the slopes on either side from the base to the rim, hunting for sentries. If the rider he trailed was the bank robber, he might have partners. Slocum was not convinced the same man who had robbed the bank had also killed Delgado's prisoner. The bank robber had run from town like a scalded dog and had left enough of a trail to tell Slocum he was miles away when the murder happened.

That meant another man in the gang might be roaming around. Nowhere did Slocum spot a guard standing watch. More cautiously than before, he entered the deep notch and felt the canyon walls rising on either side, crowding in until he could have touched either wall by simply reaching out. His horse shied more now, jumping at every sound. Taking as much time as needed, he soothed his horse to keep it quiet. A loud neigh would echo up the canyon and alert who-ever was cooking.

The scent of cooking made Slocum's mouth water and re-minded him how long it had been since he had eaten. He pushed on. The sooner he caught the outlaw responsible for robbing Williams's bank, the faster he could move on.

The canyon walls fell away and widened into a sere valley dotted with stunted trees. The oppressive heat from the narrow passage died down a little, but it was still desert country. The heat boiling off the acres of rock assured him of that.

He turned slowly, nose in the air like a prairie dog. He could make out the scent of roasting meat now and turned his horse in that direction. Without an idea how far he had to go, Slocum slowed to a walk and then began stopping every few minutes to study the ground around him. When he saw a sin-gle set of hoofprints going in the same direction, he knew he was close.

Loosening the leather thong keeper over the hammer of his Colt Navy, he readied himself for what might turn into a gunfight.

Barely twenty yards closer to the campfire, he heard a horse ahead. From the noise, he knew the horse was being saddled in a hurry. Slocum put his heels to his own horse and shot forward. He whipped out his six-shooter and burst through a stand of trees into a sandy spit where a fire sput-tered and burned. Dangling over it was what remained of a slab of venison.

"Where . . . ?" Slocum looked around for the man who had been in this campsite a few seconds earlier.

The shot rang out and took his horse out from under him. This had happened before during the bank robbery, and Slocum had been trapped beneath deadweight. Kicking free as the horse collapsed allowed Slocum to hit the ground and roll away. He frantically sought the sniper.

All he heard was the sizzle and pop of grease dripping into the fire and the soft wind sneaking through distant trees. He got to his feet and went to his horse.

"Son of a bitch. Somebody's out to kill every last damn horse the judge owns," he said. The bullet had caught the horse just above the leg, had drilled through both lungs and had come out the far side. Slocum looked around but the shooter was long gone. He set to work getting his saddle and other gear free of the horse.

"It's going to be a long walk back to Dry Water," he said aloud, then dropped his saddle beside the fire. "Might as well have something to eat." He tore into the haunch of venison. Whoever the unseen horse killer was, he had left behind a tasty piece of cooked meat.

5

The heat hammered at Slocum until he staggered. Every step became more than a chore. He peered up at the cloudless blue California sky. All he saw was the harsh sun.

"Gotta find shade," he said to himself. His mouth was filled with cotton because he had finished the last of the water in his canteen more than an hour earlier. "Walk at night."

He stumbled and fell to his knees. As his head bent forward, he felt the sun against his neck. It was almost peaceful, soothing, the warm caress of a lover. Slocum jerked awake when he realized he had fallen face forward into the ground. He pulled bloodied shards of stone from his cheek and chin and rolled to his side. The sun burned at his face and felt worse than the rocks that had sliced his face.

He pulled his hat down and rested for a moment, but he knew he could not stay. He got to his feet, dropped his saddle and saddlebags, then staggered toward the side of the canyon for the pitiful shade it offered. He crashed into solid rock and slithered down onto his knees. Turning, he sat heavily, his feet thrust out in the middle of the passage. After rubbing his eyes a couple times to clear them, he wondered where the hell he was. Once he'd finished the tasty venison, he had tried to follow the tracks back to the far side of the pass he had just traversed. Somewhere along the way, the heat had burned its way into his brain and confused him.

He didn't have the slightest idea where the hell he was.

"Where the hell?" he muttered. "I'm in hell. No, can't." He shook his head. "Hell can't be this damn hot."

Slocum dozed and snapped awake when a cold wind blew across him. Wiping at the caked blood on his face sent pain angling into his body. This spurred him to get to his feet. Shaky, Slocum looked around and tried to get his bearings. Somehow, he had gotten lost in the maze of canyons leading to the campsite he had found so easily earlier in the day, guided by the scent of cooking meat. From his location at the bottom of the canyon, he could not see the stars well enough to get his bearings.

He was somewhere south of Dry Water. He had to find the North Star and head straight for it. On shaky legs, he started walking until he found a winding path to the canyon rim. Every step was agony but Slocum kept moving, struggling, fighting for every inch. Before his strength entirely vanished, he flopped on the canyon rim with a clear view of the night sky.

Sitting cross-legged, Slocum began locating the constellations he knew. When he found the Big Dipper, his heart skipped a beat. He followed the pointer stars to his beacon in the night.

"East," he said in wonder. "I went east when I got lost." Somehow he had kept going in the same direction he had ridden as he approached the cooking fire before the sniper killed his horse.

Slocum spent another hour making sure he had his bearings and figured out his best route north. Walking at night meant cooler and even cold temperatures. He began to shiver after he had been stumbling along for an hour. But when he got down off the canyon rim and found the trail he had originally followed, he knew he could reach the watering hole before sunrise.

Footsore and tired to the bone, Slocum dived into the pool of cold, bracing water soon after the sun poked over the mountains he had just left. He drank his fill, soaked his feet and rested up. He had hopes that Marshal Delgado might come hunting for him, but there were no travelers coming to the watering hole. As night dropped on the desert again, Slocum knew he had to keep moving. He had drunk his fill of the sweet water and felt strong enough to make it to Dry Water.

He was hobbling by the time he reached town. His vision was blurred and he hoped he had found the right place. In the distance he heard a curious buzz like he had kicked over a beehive.

"Slocum? What happened?"

"Need a drink." Slocum got the words out. To his surprise, a shot glass brimming with whiskey appeared in his hand as if by magic. He knocked back the potent liquor and felt it kick him like a mule.

"That's a dime."

"What?"

"I said, that's a dime. You want credit? I kin do that, but you got to get the judge to guarantee I'll git my money."

"Alton?"

"Who the hell else do you think'd be givin' you rotgut whiskey?"

Slocum saw that he was seated in the Desert Oasis. The empty glass in front of him and the burning taste on his lips assured him he was not hallucinating. He had stumbled into the town saloon and been served a drink by the barkeep.

"What about the marshal?"

"What about him? He got back yesterday with Cal Bennigan. I declare, that man's crazy as a bedbug. Don't blame the marshal one bit for putting shackles on him to get him into jail."

"I found him," Slocum said. He tried to get everything square in his head but couldn't. He needed sleep and food and more whiskey. The latter he got after asking twice, but Alton had yet to put out the day's lunch.

"Who'd you find, Slocum?"

Turning in his chair, Slocum saw Roger Williams loom-ing above him.

"I heard-tell you were back. You didn't . . . do as I asked concerning Bennigan."

"The robber," Slocum said. "I found him."

"Where? Did you capture him?"

"Slocum walked in all by his lonesome," Alton told the banker.

"Then you killed him?"

"Shot my horse out from under," Slocum croaked out. He needed another shot of whiskey.

"You shot his horse?"

"No, no, he shot my horse. I had to walk back."

"Hell, Slocum, you mean you walked in that heat? You must be some kind of iron man." Alton poured another shot. "If you're tellin' the truth and not funnin' us all, that one's on me. You still got to pay for the first one, though."

"Look at his condition man," Williams snapped. "He wouldn't lie about a thing like that." The banker shook him. "Did you kill the robber?"

"No," Slocum said. "Never even saw him. Shot my horse. Actually, the horse belongs to Judge Tunstell."

"Let him be, Roger." The judge suddenly came into view.

"You weren't the one robbed, Judge," Williams said an-grily. "I want to find out what went on out there."

"Delgado has told you all you need to know. Now get out of here so I can talk to Mr. Slocum. He is my employee, af-ter all."

"You can't do this, Judge. I want to know about the rob-ber. Where he is. If he's dead."

"Don't know where he is. Alive. He's more alive 'n me," Slocum slurred. The saloon spun in crazy circles around him. For a brief moment, he focused on the judge's hatchet-thin face. Then he passed out.

Slocum awoke with a start. Nothing was right around him. He sat up and heard a crinkly sound. Looking down, he saw he was in a bed with starched linen sheets. Shifting his weight slightly, he realized he was in a bed with a feather mattress.

"So you finally decided to wake up. Have a good sleep?"

"I reckon I've died and gone to heaven," Slocum said, looking toward the door. Judge Tunstell stood there, looking smug.

"You ought to be, doing a damn fool thing like walking back. How far did you carry your saddle before you dropped it?"

"Halfway," Slocum said. "It'd be a pity to lose that saddle."

Tunstell chuckled, then sobered. "You lost another of my fine horses, didn't you?"

"Shot out from under me, like before. Might be the same yahoo did it. I never caught sight of him."

"This is a serious matter, Mr. Slocum. You are not a careless person. You never saw the man who shot at you?"

"Shot at the horse," Slocum corrected. "If he had wanted to kill me, it was an easy shot. He hit what he was aiming at."

"So he only wanted you on foot. That still does nothing to recompense me for the loss of a second horse. He must be brought to justice before my court."

"Can't say I didn't try. He must have spotted me coming, though I don't know how. Might be that he has an accomplice."

"Two, one, what's the difference? He—they—are killers and must be brought to justice."

"If he robbed the bank and got away with that much money, why is he within a hundred miles of Dry Water? Any robber worth his salt would be riding hard to get away from the law, especially with ten thousand dollars bouncing in his saddlebags."

"That is a considerable amount of money. Could one man carry that much in his saddlebags?" Tunstell wondered aloud. He waved it off. "That's of no import. Since you are feeling better, the marshal wants a word with you. I won't let him bother you too long. You need your rest."

"Are you a doctor and a judge?"

Tunstell laughed at this. "You do amuse me, Mr. Slocum. I consider you my work in progress. You are destined for bigger things, if only you live to see them." The judge turned and snapped his fingers. As if waiting for the command, Marshal Delgado appeared in the hall. "Don't be too long, Marshal." Tunstell stepped back and Slocum heard the judge's steady tread down a flight of stairs.

"You look a world better, Slocum," the marshal said.

"Where am I? This place is mighty fancy." Slocum took the opportunity to look around for the first time. The bed was posh but the furnishings were rich. A cut-crystal decanter stood on the cherrywood chest of drawers. An imposing wardrobe dominated the wall behind the door. A fancy glass doorknob glinted as a ray of sunlight somehow found it and was refracted. The thick pile rug on the floor totally swallowed the sound of the marshal's boots as he came closer to the bed.

"Upstairs at the courthouse. This here's part of the judge's quarters."

"The county surely does well by its judicial staff," Slocum said.

"Better than it does by its law enforcement. I asked for a five-dollar-a-month raise and the mayor laughed at me." Delgado grabbed a chair and pulled it over to the side of the bed. "Tell me about the robber."

Slocum related what had happened and his lack of identification.

"Who else would try to shoot you out of the saddle without so much as a 'Howdy, stranger' when you rode up?"

"You might be right or it could be some suspicious son of a bitch," Slocum said. "Are you going out to find him?"

Slocum pulled back the covers and swung his legs around. They felt like lead, but he was in good enough condition to ride. "Let me get my boots."

"The judge would skin me alive if I let you ride with me," Delgado said. "I know this place. I will go after the robber and bring him back."

Slocum wondered if it was braggadocio on the marshal's part, if he wanted the reward Williams had offered all for himself, or if he still felt guilty about having a prisoner murdered in his jail.

"I can go, but I'll need a horse."

"Don't even try to stand up," warned the marshal. Slocum tried anyway and fell hard. Delgado helped him back into bed. "Your feet are all blistered from walking and your legs wobbled like they were made from rubber. A day or two and you'll be fine."

"Wait for me, then," Slocum said.

"I need to do this, Slocum," Delgado said softly.

"He's good," Slocum said. "Whoever it is you're after is damned good." Slocum wasn't much for bragging, but anyone who could get the drop on him that easily without being seen had to be about the best. Riding blindly into an ambush was one thing. A man couldn't be faulted for that if he had no inkling it was coming. Slocum had known the man was camped out and eating his meal. His approach to the camp had been cautious, and he had been alert and ready. That hadn't mattered.

"I'd take a posse but nobody's willing to go with me."

"Deputize a few of them over at the Desert Oasis. Like you did me."

"They'd fall out of their saddles dead drunk within a mile," Delgado said, shaking his head. "I will do fine on my own."

"And?"

"And you must tend my prisoner."

"Bennigan?"

"He never stops swearing. Most men would have repeated themselves by now, but not old Cal. He is more inventive than I had given him credit for being."

"I'm still deputized? Is that why I get to be his wet nurse?"

"You cut right to the heart of the matter, Slocum. The judge has authorized it. You still work for him, but he is loaning you to the town for jailhouse duty while I am gone."

Slocum thought that job might be more dangerous than

trying to track down the ghostly bank robber out in the hills bordering the Mojave Desert. He remembered vividly how the banker had offered money to kill Calvin Bennigan. Slocum doubted the banker had the grit to shoot the miner himself, but keeping the prisoner safe might be more difficult than tracking down the bank robber out in the desert.

The marshal had barely gone when Tunstell returned.

"Your clothes are in the wardrobe. You ought to hobble on over to the jailhouse and watch the prisoner."

Slocum considered mentioning Williams's offer to the judge, then decided against it. He had told Delgado. If the marshal had mentioned it, Tunstell knew. If not, Slocum decided it was none of his business how the political power was spread around Dry Water.

"I'll need my six-gun," Slocum said, rummaging through the wardrobe and not finding it or his gun belt.

"I have it under lock and key downstairs. Courthouse rules. Nobody carries iron up here into my quarters. I'll have it ready for you as you leave." Tunstell paused and frowned. "Are you expecting trouble at the jail?"

"Never hurts to be prepared," Slocum said. But he expected more than a little trouble if Williams took it into his head to plug Bennigan.

6

Slocum was going stir-crazy. He grabbed the iron bars of the cell and shook hard enough to rattle the door. Cal Bennigan opened one eye and glared at him.

"Why don't ya give it a rest, Slocum? I'm tryin' to sleep."

"Shut up," Slocum snapped. He stepped away from the cell door and stared at his prisoner. How many times he had been the prisoner and the jailer had taunted him, he could not remember. It wasn't as if he was taunting Bennigan. He wasn't. He felt more trapped than his prisoner, though. Two days. Marshal Delgado had been gone for two days. Slocum's feet felt better—and they were getting itchy in more than one way.

The healing helped make them itchy, but there was also the need for him to move on. He had stayed in Dry Water too long. The judge and marshal thought nothing of trusting him with a prisoner, of being a deputy, of delivering legal papers. He was downright respectable. That bothered him less than the feeling of invisible ropes hog-tying him. The more they expected from him, the less freedom he had. Soon enough he would be hunting for a permanent place to stay and become a member of the community.

"What did you do that they wanted you off your claim?" Slocum asked.

48

"Keep askin' them damn fool questions and someday you might catch me at a weak spot and I'd tell ya," Bennigan said. He rolled over, face to the wall. Within a few minutes he was snoring gently. Slocum looked up at the barred cell window and knew it would be hard for anyone to stick a six-shooter in and hit Bennigan. Only if the man walked out into the middle of the small cell and exposed himself would any gunman have a clean shot at him. If that happened, Slocum knew he would hear and come running.

Like a dog whose master called it.

Slocum hated being in the marshal's office more every hour.

He went to the desk in the small outer office, sat in Delgado's chair and hiked his boots to the desktop. He ought to catch a few winks like Bennigan, but somehow his mind kept turning over everything that had happened since his first horse had been shot out from under him. If Delgado captured the lone bank robber and got him to talk, it would explain a lot of what made no sense to Slocum. His curiosity had gotten him into more trouble than he could remember, but finding answers always felt right, even if the result had not always been good.

Before he could ponder too long, the door creaked open and Mayor Grierson came bustling in.

"There you are, Slocum. I might have known you'd be sitting with your feet up on the desk, doing nothing."

"Don't have anything to do but watch the prisoner," Slocum said. He made no move to drop his feet from the desktop. Claude Grierson might be mayor, but he wasn't Slocum's boss.

"You do now. Just got a wire from over in Pemberton that the new schoolmarm's arrived and needs transport back to Dry Water."

Slocum had been thrown off the train in Pemberton. It had been chance that Judge Tunstell had also been on the platform and overheard his plight. That had started his tale of woe in Dry Water when Tunstell had offered him a job and he had taken it.

"So?"

"So get your feet off the desk and get your ass over to Pemberton. It'd be good if you could get her back before sundown so we can see that she gets all settled in at the boardinghouse."

"I don't have a horse," Slocum said, thinking that he could take Conchita. The swaybacked nag was in a corral out back. Conchita might have been the most accommodating horse he had ever ridden.

"Take my buggy. It's outside. Don't abuse the horse or I'll see you locked up alongside Bennigan!"

"Who's going to watch Bennigan?" Slocum wondered if the mayor and banker might be in cahoots to kill the miner. Then he remembered how Williams and Grierson had argued so bitterly. Still, what snippets of that argument he had caught must have involved Bennigan.

"I'll take a stint. Morris, the judge's clerk, can come over later and watch. He can do his work here as easily as he can at the courthouse," Grierson said. "Not that I see Morris doing a powerful lot of work anytime, but I can't get the judge to fire him."

"How'll I know her?" Slocum gingerly lowered his feet and stood. He walked just fine, but now and then got a twinge from a popped blister. At least his legs were once more up to supporting his weight.

"How many women will be sitting on the railroad depot platform waiting for you?"

"Could be a fair number," Slocum said deadpan. Grierson started to reply, realized he was being joshed, then motioned for Slocum to get out and on the road to Pemberton.

The buggy was parked where Grierson had said. Slocum heaved a sigh, got in and took the reins. He preferred riding to driving, but the town's new schoolteacher was likely to be older than dirt and ugly to boot. Who else would come to an out-of-the-way hellhole next to the Mojave Desert at the ass end of summer?

He snapped the reins and the horse obediently began pulling. Slocum eventually got to the fork in the road and turned west this time, heading toward Pemberton and away from the hills where he had lost his last horse. He noted how rocky the terrain became and how poorly the buggy went over the bumpy road. More than once the road narrowed to only inches from a sharp drop-off into an arroyo. The horse plodded along, and Slocum began to sweat as much from the fear of falling into one of those deep ravines as from the sun beating down on his head.

It took better than three hours for him to reach Pemberton. Finding the railroad station was easy enough, but Slocum considered stopping off at one of the saloons lined along a row in town. Dry Water had only one saloon. Slocum didn't mind Alton and his stale jokes, but his whiskey left something to be desired. Whether Alton used too much nitric acid or not enough rusty nails to give his whiskey bite and body, Slocum didn't know. He was thirsty for a shot of rotgut that wouldn't rip out his throat on the way down.

But he felt a strong obligation not to let an old woman sit in this heat too long. She might keel over and have to be revived—or never revive at all. Dry Water would have to find a new schoolmarm.

Slocum steered the buggy to the front of the depot, fixed the reins and got out. He went around to the side and slowly climbed the steps to the platform. His feet protested a little, but his legs were strong and he reached the top of the six steps. He heaved a deep sigh. Dressed in a black dress with white lace collar, hands folded primly in her lap, was a woman at least seventy years old. Slocum went to her, touched the brim of his hat and said, "I'm here to take you to Dry Water, ma'am."

Rheumy eyes peered up at him. Her lips pursed as if she had bitten into a sour persimmon.

"Who are you?"

"Name's Slocum, ma'am. The mayor sent me."

"Whatever are you going on about, young man? I don't know any Dry Water and the only mayor I know is back in Tennessee."

Slocum frowned. "Mayor Grierson, over in Dry Water. You're the town's new schoolmarm, aren't you?"

"I am not. I have come to visit my no-good son and his whore of a wife. They have left me stewing on this platform for the better part of two hours."

"She's going to a ranch about an hour out of Pemberton, Mr. Slocum."

"She's not the Dry Water schoolteacher?" Slocum turned to see who had supplied all the information. His mouth opened and then snapped closed. The woman in front of him was everything the old lady impatiently waiting for her family was not.

She was tall, almost five-foot-six, and had the most abundant mane of chestnut-colored hair Slocum had ever laid eyes on. Her green eyes rivaled his as being the closest to emerald in color. She had a heart-shaped face, or maybe the widow's peak in her lustrous hair only suggested that. Lips of pure red twitched with just a hint of laughter.

"I'm Angela Enwright," she said, holding out a gloved hand. Slocum took it, wondering if he was supposed to kiss it or shake it. He wouldn't have been too outraged if she expected him to kiss it. There wasn't much of the lovely woman's body he wouldn't mind kissing.

He shook her hand.

"Pleased to meet you, Miss Enwright."

"Pleased, Mr. Slocum, or surprised?" This time a smile lit up her face in a way rivaling the sun in brilliance.

"Both. Do you have any luggage?" Slocum looked around but did not see any.

"The porter on the train said there was no way of telling where my trunk is. They will look for it, but I have little hope it will ever be found. I am afraid I have what I'm wearing— and whatever the town can supply me with until my salary allows me to purchase more."

"That's a shame," Slocum said. He tipped his hat to the old woman, who glared at him, then offered his arm to Angela Enwright and went back down the steps. Somehow, having such a lovely woman on his arm took away all the pain in his feet and put a spring in his step that had been missing since he had his second horse shot out from under him.

"Would you care for something to eat before we go to Dry Water?"

"I . . . that would be nice, but I am in a hurry to see my new home. Tell me all about it, Mr. Slocum."

"Call me John."

"And you must call me Angela," she said, smiling brightly. "Of course, not in public or where the children might overhear."

"Of course," he said, helping her into the buggy. Slocum swung in and gripped the reins. The horse gave a nervous start, causing the buggy to lurch. Angela grabbed his arm and held on as he regained control.

"I'm not used to either the horse or the buggy," Slocum explained.

"That's all right. I was not put out in the least."

Slocum felt her hand linger on his arm. She moved away reluctantly and then stared directly ahead.

"It is quite hot out here, isn't it?"

"What part of the country you from, Angela? I don't recognize your accent."

"I surely do yours, John. From the South. Wait, don't tell me. Let me guess. I'd say the Carolinas or, perhaps, yes, I have it. Georgia. You hail from Georgia, don't you?"

"I do," he said. "It's been a spell since I was back there. Since the war."

"I didn't mean to pry. I know how difficult the war was for so many Southerners. But you must tell me about Dry Water. Every detail. Don't leave out a thing."

"I've only come to town a few weeks back," Slocum said. He knew nothing about the school or the children. The men he had seen most were the ones who frequented the town saloon. For all that time he spent in the Desert Oasis, he had never once partaken of the two soiled doves who sometimes hovered about until Alton chased them off. Slocum guessed the barkeep's reluctance to allow them in his drinking emporium came less from distaste for their profession than not getting a share of their revenue. The men they left with seldom returned to drink more that night. Alton had to see the two women as a minus when it came to counting up the night's take.

"Oh, don't worry about the children and church and things like that, John," Angela said after he had run dry on what he knew. "Tell me about the bank. And I understand Dry Water has one of the finest courthouses in this part of California. What of the judge and the marshal?"

Slocum found this curious, but riding with such a pretty girl pressed up close beside him on the hard buggy seat loosened his tongue.

"Shot in the jailhouse! How awful," she said after he told her of Delgado's disgrace over losing a prisoner. Something about her tone made Slocum study her more closely. There was a sharpness to her protest that did not ring true.

"You don't need to worry about such things," Slocum said. "The marshal keeps the peace so the townsfolk don't even know about most crime going on." He realized this made it sound as if Marshal Delgado was involved in the crime, or that there was a considerable amount of thievery going on that the marshal covered up.

He smiled ruefully as that thought struck him. There well might be corruption in the town. Judge Tunstell was far more prosperous than a county judge had any right being, and the courthouse was about the prettiest building Slocum had seen since the time he had been in St. Louis. Whatever went on between the mayor and banker was not open and aboveboard, either, and he had yet to figure out why Tunstell had been so eager to throw Cal Bennigan into jail and seize his property. From everything Slocum had learned from the land assessor, Bennigan's mine was barely producing enough gold to keep the man alive. That was more than most of the mines in his area produced, but no one was getting rich from the mining.

"How long until we reach Dry Water?" Angela asked

after they had been on the trail an hour. "I'm getting mighty thirsty."

"Sorry," Slocum said. "I thought the mayor had tossed a canteen into the back. I never checked before I set out. And I should have made sure we had water back in Pemberton."

"I suppose you are used to going for long periods of time without water. You have the look of being a very tough hombre. That's the expression, isn't it? *Hombre*?"

He saw how she glanced in the direction of the worn butt of his Colt Navy.

"It is," Slocum said. "Be careful with Spanish words you might pick up around town, though. Some of them might not be fit for a lady's ears, much less her lips."

"Oh, John," she said, laughing. The laughter faded as the buggy lurched violently.

Slocum drew back on the reins. They were on a stretch of road where the shoulder dropped off abruptly into a ravine. He had been cautious in this stretch going to Pemberton, but now the buggy was heavier. Every rock they ran over caused a hard jolt.

"Whoa, whoa!" Slocum half stood to get better leverage pulling back on the reins, but the horse was having none of it. Rearing, the horse lashed out with its hooves. This caused the buggy to twist sideways a mite.

"John!"

This was the last thing Slocum heard before the wheel came off the buggy, and they pitched over the side of the road and began rolling down the steep incline.

7

The world swung by faster and faster as Slocum rolled down the hillside. He came to a sudden stop when he crashed into a boulder. He gasped, tried to stand and sank back down to regain his strength. Pain lanced through him, but he fought it and got to his feet.

"Angela!" He looked around for the woman but didn't see her. He called again. This time he heard a faint moan. He hobbled a few feet down the ravine, turned and looked up it. The dry bed was empty save for a lizard scurrying away as fast as its thin legs could carry it.

Slocum looked up the slope and saw the woman halfway up. From the way she struggled, her skirts had caught on a cactus or rock. Whatever it was supporting her, if she succeeded in getting free, she'd come tumbling down after him.

"Don't move. Don't try to get free. I'll get to you." Saying it was easier than doing it. The loose rock on the slope made the footing treacherous. Slocum scraped his knees and hands as he fought every inch of the way back up to where he could see what had halted Angela's slide down the hill.

"You're caught on a rock. If your skirt starts to tear, you're in for quite a fall."

"Down to where you already were," she said. She groaned,

56

then lay on her back staring up at the cloudless blue sky. "It's not my skirt that's caught. It's my bustle."

Slocum almost laughed. Angela was more embarrassed about how she was caught than the fact that she was trapped. He edged closer, keeping his footing. One slip and he would tumble back down the slope. As banged up as he was, Slocum was not sure he could muster the strength to get up the hill again. He grasped the woman's hand and tugged, trying to get her to stand. She was too firmly caught. Working his fingers under the cloth, he traced the intricate wire frame of her bustle.

"It's jammed between two rocks," Slocum said. "I can't tug hard enough to get it free without sending both of us into the arroyo."

"Very well," Angela said with a sigh of resignation. "Let me extricate myself."

"What?"

"I will get out of this damned bustle!"

"Oh, sorry," Slocum said. "Do you need any help?"

"I . . . no, thank you, John. Not this time." Their eyes locked. If Angela's position hadn't been so precarious, Slocum would have kissed her. As it was, he only turned and balanced the best he could.

Listening to her grunt and strain and finally break free required all his control not to turn and watch. When he heard something sliding downhill, he cast a quick look. The wire frame of the bustle tumbled over and over into the ravine.

"There," Angela said. "Free."

He turned back. Except for the removal of the delightful posterior feminine implement, she looked no different. He held out his hand. She took it for balance and began digging the toes of her shoes into the hard ground to gain traction. Together they finally got back to the road.

Angela wiped sweat and grime from her face, using a handkerchief. Slocum had no idea where she had hidden it. He used his filthy bandanna to perform the same act of aggressive sweat removal on his own face. He wrung out the bandanna and tied it back around his neck. By the time he was finished, she had made her lacy hanky disappear again.

"What do we do now?"

"We won't be going anywhere in the buggy, that's for sure," Slocum said. He examined the buggy and saw how the wheel had popped free of its axle and gone rolling downhill just before he had followed. Even if he was so inclined, retrieving the wheel would do no good. The axle had broken when the wheel came off.

"It might be a good thing my trunk was not to be found on the train," Angela said. "Carrying it without use of the buggy would be quite difficult."

Slocum looked up into the sun and squinted. Lugging a woman's trunk would be impossible. He said nothing to her about that, though. Let her keep her fine Eastern ways. Soon enough she would discover that life on the frontier was more difficult than she imagined.

"We're about the same distance from Pemberton and Dry Water," Slocum said. "The way back to Pemberton is rockier and there are more hills."

"So pressing on to Dry Water will be an easier hike?" she asked.

Slocum nodded. It hardly mattered which direction they went, except that going forward would get them where they wanted to go. If he returned to Pemberton, he would have to wire Grierson and let the man know what had happened. Angela would have to be put up in a hotel until someone else rode out to fetch her back to Dry Water. He figured they saved a whole passel of people trouble by completing their trip.

"Should we wait for the sun to go down and walk in the dark? You are looking a mite peaked," she said. Angela put a hand on his forehead. Slocum drew back.

"What are you doing?"

"I wanted to be sure you were not running a fever. That is a sign of heatstroke."

"It is hot," Slocum said, "but we might find that luck is

with us if we can stop anyone riding this road and send word
to Grierson."

"Who?"

"The mayor of Dry Water."

"Oh, I . . . misheard you. Of course I know Mayor Grierson."

"He hired you, didn't he?"

"Why, look, John. Birds." Angela pointed to the sky
where buzzards circled in lazy downward spirals. Slocum
wasn't sure if they were the birds' obvious dinner or if something else had already died out in the desert.

"Let me hike to the top of that rise and see," he said.
"Stay here. If you can find some shade, sit in it."

"There are other things I would rather sit on," Angela said.

Slocum hesitated, wondering at her meaning. The way
she looked at him was much like the way those circling buzzards looked at something about to die. He shrugged it off and
began making his way up a low rise. It took longer than he expected, but when he got to the ridge he was able to look down
along the road all the way to the fork leading off to Dry Water.

"Hey, here! Can you give us some help?" Slocum waved
to a rider approaching the fork from the opposite direction.
He worried that he was too far away to be heard. Then he
worried that he was not out of rifle range. The rider drew a
Winchester from a saddle scabbard and fired several times at
Slocum. The distance was too great for there to be much
chance of Slocum being hit, but the man's intent was obvious. When the gunman realized he was not going to hit
Slocum, he wheeled his horse about and galloped away in a
thick cloud of dust. By the time it had settled and Slocum
was able to get an unobstructed view of the road, the rider
had disappeared.

In the same direction taken by the bank robber when he
had fled Dry Water.

Slocum went back down the hill to where Angela sat in
the dubious shade of the overturned buggy.

"John, I thought I heard shots. Are you all right?"

"A rider mistook me for a coyote," he said. "Doesn't look as if we'll get much help from him."

"He shot at you? How could he ever mistake you for an animal?" She stared wide-eyed at him when realization hit her. "He wanted to shoot *you*."

"Lucky he was a poor shot," Slocum said. He considered all that they could do. Hiking along the road to the fork and then into Dry Water looked a tad more dangerous than it had a few minutes earlier. Heat and dehydration presented dangers. A man with blood in his eye and a decent rifle was another matter.

"What are we going to do?"

Slocum put his finger to his lips to silence her. Angela started to ask why, then turned her head and caught the same sound Slocum already had.

"A horse?"

"Ours," Slocum said. "Stay here. I'll be back in a few minutes with our ride to town."

"But—"

Slocum ignored her protests as he set off to capture the horse that had pulled the buggy all the way to Pemberton and halfway back to Dry Water. Whatever had spooked it and caused it to rear was long gone. Slocum rounded the hill where he had spied the rider, and at the base stood his horse. Rather than walk up to it, Slocum sat on a hot rock and waited for the animal to notice him. The horse was still frightened. If it took off at a gallop, it might kill itself from exhaustion, long before Slocum could grab it.

After a few minutes, the horse decided Slocum was no real threat. It moved toward him. He still sat motionless. Only when it was within arm's reach did Slocum stand. The horse tried to shy away, but it was too late. Slocum grabbed the dangling, torn reins and hung on, keeping the horse from rearing. It took a few more minutes to gentle the horse, and then it allowed itself to be led as docile as a lamb back to where Angela was still sitting in the shade of the buggy.

"Riding sure beats walking in this sun," Slocum said.

"What am I to do? I cannot ride that. I don't know how."

"There's nothing to it," Slocum said. "I reckon it's about time for the schoolmarm to do some learning."

He swung up onto the horse. Riding bareback wasn't that much more difficult for him. Slocum reached down. Angela looked skeptically at his extended hand, then took it and let him pull her up behind him. It took some doing for her to get her skirts settled, but once she did, Slocum felt she was securely seated.

"Good seat," he said.

"Why, thank you."

She put her arms around his waist and clung tightly, making him wonder if they each meant the same thing. At the moment, he did not much care if she thought he complimented her fine ass or how she was riding. They trotted along the road until Slocum saw a way off the road.

He veered sharply from the twin ruts that marked the road to the fork and cut across country.

"Why have you left the road, John? Is this a shortcut?"

"Might be shorter," Slocum said.

"But it's something else. What are you not telling me about the man who shot at you?"

"Could be a robber wanted by the law," Slocum said. He had not been able to get a good enough look to even see the man's shirt. "By getting off the road, we can avoid him."

"Did he want to rob you? Why didn't he pursue the matter and finish you off?"

A million answers raced through Slocum's mind but none of them were likely to put Angela's fears to rest.

"You don't have to put sugar on it for me," she said, as if his thoughts were being shouted from the tops of every mountain in California. "There's trouble brewing. I want to know. I deserve to know what I'm getting myself into."

"There was a bank robbery a week or so back," Slocum said. "Two robbers were killed and a third got away with a pile of money. The man who shot at me is likely the third robber."

"Why would a robber stay where he committed such a robbery?" she asked. Slocum felt her arms around him begin to tremble.

"That's been worrying me something fierce," Slocum said. "There's no doubt somebody's out for blood." He told her how he had lost two horses to gunfire and had to walk back to Dry Water.

Her reaction surprised him. She laughed out loud.

"You have the worst luck, John. Two horses, a long walk, now the buggy loses a wheel and you're having to ride double to Dry Water."

"I don't see that as being such bad luck," Slocum said. He was rewarded with Angela tightening her arms around his waist. It might have been the uneven gait of the horse or it might have been something else, but Angela's hands moved downward from his waist until they pressed in just above his groin. He felt stirrings there that became downright uncomfortable.

"We should camp, John," she said after they had ridden a spell.

"We can get to Dry Water in another hour or two."

"I . . . I'm not used to riding a horse like this. I really need to rest. My legs feel like they are going to fall off if I don't get to just stand on solid ground."

"We can take a rest," he said. "Then—"

"Camp," Angela insisted. "I have had a very taxing day."

"Don't have the equipment to camp." He had left his saddle somewhere up in the hills to the east, and Mayor Grierson had not seen fit to include much in the way of gear in the buggy. There had been no reason.

"We can build a fire. We can make do for one night."

"No blankets," he pointed out.

"You're not opposed to sharing body heat, are you?"

There was a boldness in her words that he responded to—in more than one way.

"Not with you," Slocum said. He looked around and saw a sandy spit sheltered from the wind. The rocks would release their heat slowly during the cold desert night, keeping them warm. A small fire would make it cozy.

"I do want something to drink, though. Is there any water around?"

Slocum relaxed his control of the horse and saw how it turned, heading for the spot he had already decided would be adequate for the night. Slocum's luck was running high again. There was a small spring nearby. He let the horse drink its fill while he gathered firewood. When he brought an armload back, Angela had dug a small fire pit and stacked rocks around it. She stood, brushed back a strand of her reddish brown hair, then put her hands on her hips.

"Did I do well?"

"Perfectly," Slocum said, dropping the wood. He started to stack some of the kindling to start a fire, then looked up at the woman.

Angela had unfastened her blouse and let the shirttails flap free in the gentle breeze blowing through the sheltering rocks. She took a deep breath. From where he knelt Slocum saw her breasts rise and fall heavily. He would have said nothing except for the hard little nubs pressing against the thin undergarment she wore. She was as excited he was.

Slocum forgot the fire and turned toward the woman. He ran his hands up under her skirts and found a warm, firm leg. Her green eyes fixed on him, hot and hungry. She licked her lips and widened her stance in obvious invitation.

His hand stroked over her calf and upward until he caressed the backs of her knees. She let out a small sigh. Slocum moved closer and ran his hands up her inner thighs. The smooth, warm flesh trembled at his touch all the way up to her crotch. He found that she did not wear any underwear. His fingers brushed through the tangled forest he found there. Her inner oils already leaked out, dousing his hands.

She gasped in pleasure when he thrust his finger into her heated slit.

"Oh, John, yes," Angela sighed. She twisted from side to

side, grinding herself down into his hand and around his impaling finger.

Slocum pushed up her skirts and exposed her bare legs to his gaze. His heart raced now. He thrust his head up under and turned to kiss the insides of her thighs. The woman quivered and shook as he worked his way up higher. His lips kissed and his tongue licked as his finger stroked in and out of her slickened interior.

By the time his mouth fastened over her nether lips, she was sagging down, unable to support herself. He followed her to the ground, his tongue lapping like a dog over the length of her gash. Her legs rose up on either side of his head. Her knees parted to more fully expose herself. Slocum heard nothing but tiny gasps as he began thrusting his tongue between her pinkly scalloped sex lips and into her heated interior.

"Oh, John, I'm on fire. You're setting me on fire."

He reached around under her and grasped her fleshy buttocks. Squeezing as he tongued her caused a quake to pass through her entire body. She hunched up off the sandy ground and shoved her crotch hard into his face. Slocum did not flinch away. He sucked and licked and kept tonguing until the earthquake of sensation had passed from her.

"You know how to treat a girl," Angela said, eyes half-closed and her voice husky.

"Do you know how to treat a man?" Slocum pushed back and stood. He had her full attention as he unbuckled his gun belt and tossed it aside. He reached down and began unbuttoning his jeans. When his erection popped out, long and hard and hot, Angela scrambled around to get onto hands and knees. She came to him, looking up past his trembling shaft.

"I know what you want," she whispered hoarsely.

"Do you now?"

"Let me show you." Rather than doing for him what he had done for her already, she pulled up her skirts even more until they were bunched around her waist. Lithely turning, she stayed on all fours and waggled her perky ass cheeks in his direction.

"Reckon you do," Slocum said, dropping behind her. He laid his hand on her curving flesh. It rippled under his fingers smooth as marble. But no cold stone had ever been this vibrantly alive. He reached around her waist and pulled her in to his groin. His hardened length slid past those half moons and went lower, parting her sex lips. She groaned in pleasure. Slocum stroked back and forth in the lust-slick channel. Then he found the exact spot where his mouth had been such a short time ago.

He pressed the thick head of his manhood against her and levered his hips forward. He sank balls-deep into her. For a moment Slocum was entirely engulfed in her tight, wet heat.

She bucked like a bronco, and Slocum had to slide his arm around her waist to hold her close. He felt her clamping down all around him, crushing him in the most pleasurable way possible. He lifted her up and got her onto her feet. Still together, Angela bent over and Slocum behind, they turned around and around. Then she reached out and braced herself against a rock.

"Do it, John, do it hard. I want it hard!"

Both hands around her hips now to give him more leverage, he began pistoning back and forth until he felt as if his cock had turned into a white-hot poker. She threw her head back and cried out again in total release. Slocum came only seconds later. He felt the rising tide within him that suddenly exploded into her grasping core.

Panting, Slocum stepped away. Angela presented such a delectable sight. Her skirts were still hiked up around her waist, leaving her naked below—all the way down to her shoes. Slocum wanted to reach out and stroke the milky white curves of her buttocks but he held back.

She looked over her shoulder at him, a satisfied look on her face.

"You don't need any more schooling," she said.

"Might be you've been a bad girl," Slocum said. He ran his hands over her now and felt her flesh tense below.

"Then you must punish me—if you're up to it." She waggled her ass again and then gasped when Slocum laid his open hand on her behind.

Slocum was up to it.

8

Slocum rode back to where Angela lay curled up beside the guttering fire. She looked up, rubbed sleep from her eyes and mumbled, "Where did you go, John?"

"Out scouting the best route," he lied. They had spent most of the night in delightful pursuits. But although he had been exhausted, a single thought kept gnawing away at him. The rider who had taken the shots at him was still out there. If the owlhoot happened upon them in their small encampment, they would be sitting ducks.

Rather than wait for the rider to find them, Slocum had gone out hunting. All he had found was a set of hoofprints leading from the fork in the road toward the distant eastern hills. The only clue as to the rider's identity was a loose horseshoe. From what Slocum could tell, the right front shoe was about ready to come loose. The only farrier he knew of in the area was in Dry Water. There might be one in Pemberton, but that was a lot longer ride, especially if the horse threw the shoe.

"I'm hungry. How long until we reach Dry Water?"

Slocum had not seen any trace of the rider, other than the tracks left in the dusty ground.

"If we ride hard, we can make it in an hour or so."

"Well, you've certainly shown me you can ride some things hard," Angela said. She sat up and ran her hands over her breasts and downward toward her crotch. Then she jumped to her feet, brushed off the sand and said, "Let's go."

Slocum reached down and caught her arm, pulling her up behind him. She rested her cheek against his shoulder. Humming softly, she clung to him as he turned his horse's head and guided the horse out of the sandy spit onto rockier ground. He cut straight for the road. For as long as he had scouted during the night, he had seen no evidence of an ambush being set for them.

In less time than he thought, they trotted into Dry Water. Angela might have been half asleep but she perked up when someone whistled. By the time they reached the courthouse, half the town was trailing along behind.

"You might as well introduce yourself," Slocum told her. "Give them a pretty speech, and they'll be eating out of your hand."

In a low whisper, Angela replied, "I'd rather have you eating somewhere else on my anatomy."

Slocum smiled. He helped her down and then quickly dropped to the ground. His feet were in better shape now, but he was glad he had not been forced to walk back.

"Where's my buggy?"

"Good to see you, too, Mayor," Slocum said, not even bothering to look at Grierson.

"Is that the new schoolteacher? She's mighty young. A whole lot younger than she seemed in her letter."

"She answered when I called her name," Slocum said. "That must mean she's your new schoolmarm."

"What happened to the buggy?" Grierson patted his horse on the head. The horse shied away from him.

"The wheel came off and threw us down into a gully. I unhitched the horse and we rode back."

"You should have been here yesterday."

"Had to take a detour," Slocum said. He didn't want

Angela's reputation besmirched because of the way they had spent the night together. "I had to be sure she wasn't harmed none by the tumble because she's not used to riding."

Grierson looked skeptical but more concerned about his buggy.

"Can you fix it? The buggy? You can take this horse, and I'll see if the judge can loan you another, you get it fixed and—"

"That'd be mighty hard, Mayor," Slocum said. "The axle broke, which is why the wheel came off. I'm a fair wheelwright, but the buggy's in poor shape, maybe more than I could fix without the proper tools." Slocum could fix it inside an hour but wanted nothing more to do with the mayor or his buggy.

"I'll see what I can do. Don't go far, Slocum. I'll need you to tell whoever I get to go do the repairs where the buggy is."

Slocum saw a worried Grierson turn and go to greet Angela Enwright. For a moment Slocum stared. A ray of sunlight came down past the bell tower on the courthouse and lit her like she was a diva on stage. Her clothing was filthy and her chestnut hair was mussed. Slocum tried to remember when he had seen a prettier filly. He couldn't. From the way Angela shook hands and spoke to the people of Dry Water, she was going to fit right in.

Slocum went up the courthouse steps and found the judge's door ajar. Tunstell wrote furiously at his desk but looked up when Slocum paused.

"Come in, Mr. Slocum. I thought that might be you returning. I had not realized Grierson had sent you on an errand until someone complained about poor Cal Bennigan screeching out his cell window that he hadn't been fed all day. Seems whoever you found to watch over him simply got up and walked off."

"It was Grierson," Slocum said. "He was supposed to stand watch. Or find someone who would while I was over in Pemberton."

"A new schoolteacher," Tunstell said, looking distant.

"It's been a while since we had one. I wrote the ad that Grierson put in the papers back East."

"Why not find a schoolmarm from around here?"

"We felt it was time for our children to broaden their horizons. I trust the journey wasn't too tiring for Miss Enwright?"

"She pretty near rode me into the ground," Slocum said.

"I can imagine," Tunstell said, snorting in disbelief. "Even in your weakened condition, a fifty-year-old woman is no match."

"Fifty?"

"Yes, Miss Enwright."

"I made the same mistake, Judge. At the Pemberton railroad depot. I thought the old lady sitting there was Miss Enwright. Turned out she was waiting for a family outside Pemberton."

"How old is Miss Enwright?" Tunstell rocked back in his chair and stared hard at Slocum.

"Not a day over thirty. Hardly that," Slocum allowed.

"Do tell. I must have misread her application to work here. I was of the impression she was an old maid schoolteacher."

"Depends on what you mean by *old maid,* I reckon," Slocum said.

"You're thinking about leaving Dry Water, aren't you, Mr. Slocum?"

"The thought had crossed my mind."

"I want to hire you as a full-time employee of the city. You'd be my assistant."

"I don't think that's a chore I'd cotton much to."

"Oh, it's only a title. You wouldn't push papers about and be responsible for hiring or firing in the court. I leave most of that to Morris. You would work directly for me, performing as a courier and bailiff, when court is in session. Marshal Delgado has been less than pleased with fulfilling such a role when he could be breaking up fights at the saloon or doing heaven alone knows what other chores."

"It's up to the marshal to keep dead animals out of the street. Delgado has been a tad remiss."

"That's so. If you worked for me, he would no longer have an excuse not to dispose of those dogs—and horses."

They dickered awhile over pay and what horse Slocum would get for his own use from the judge's remuda. What finally won Slocum over to the notion of staying in Dry Water awhile longer was the sound of Angela's voice as she addressed the crowd gathered on the courthouse steps.

"I'm settled in quite well, thank you, Mr. Slocum," Angela said. She looked around. Her landlady busied herself with cross-stitching, but both of them knew the woman was alert for any trace of impropriety. That was why Grierson had suggested that Angela would be right at home in this boardinghouse. Any action Mrs. Harmon thought was wrong would be corrected immediately.

"Clothing? You ever hear about that missing trunk of yours?"

"I'm afraid the railroad claims no knowledge of it," Angela said. She tipped her head slightly, hinting that they should go outside. Slocum thought hard for some pretext.

"Have you seen the judge's new horse? I've tethered it right outside. Ever since you said you were interested in breeding, I've been wanting to show it to you."

Mrs. Harmon looked up quizzically from her needlework. "Why, my dear, I didn't know you were interested in horses."

"Oh, yes. The only ones I saw back East were pulling trolley cars. I think they are splendid-looking animals." As if coming to a sudden decision, Angela said, "Show me, Mr. Slocum. I would like to see the judge's prize stud."

Mrs. Harmon's attention snapped back.

"That is what you call a stallion, isn't it, Mr. Slocum?" Angela stood with her back to the landlady. Her hand pressed down on Slocum's crotch. "I do so need to learn all these terms if I am to teach the children."

"A gelding," Slocum said. "If you want to see it more closely, come on out." Slocum looked around Angela and tipped his hat in the landlady's direction. Mrs. Harmon smiled at him but did not turn back to her needlework. Slocum knew she would come to the window and watch to be sure nothing untoward went on with her newest boarder and the drifter working for the judge.

Outside, Angela said, "She is stifling me. I do declare, she wants to run my life every moment of the day."

"Small towns are like that," Slocum said.

"I've noticed that," Angela said. "Why, think of the mayor and that banker and what they're up to."

Slocum looked at her and frowned. "What might that be?"

"You know. You're just too much of a gentleman to mention such wrongdoing." Angela looked at him wide-eyed. "The bank. Those land claims. You know."

"Don't reckon I do, though there is something peculiar about how the judge sighted in on Calvin Bennigan's claim. Said there hadn't been taxes paid on it. I checked at the land office. Bennigan wasn't supposed to pay for another four months, but someone had erased the date and made it look like he was two months in arrears."

"Bennigan, you say?"

"The gent locked up in the jail."

"Where is the marshal?" Angela asked, changing the subject suddenly.

"Can't say. He went after the third bank robber, but I doubt he will have much luck."

"Why's that?"

"You surely do take an interest in everything, don't you?" Slocum looked at her. Angela was intent on what he had to say. He wondered why that might be. Most women showed little interest in politics.

"Roger Williams is making it worth his while to bring in the last robber. The marshal wants the owlhoot because of what happened in the jail to his other prisoner. It was the only time Delgado has lost a prisoner in his custody."

"The judge is an important man. What's his part in all this?"

"I don't know that there is an *all this* in Dry Water. When do you begin teaching?"

"Tomorrow morning bright and early," Angela said. "I'm not looking forward to it."

"Don't expect the kids to, either," Slocum said. This produced a chuckle from the woman.

"You're good for me, John. I want to be good for you, too."

"We're being watched," Slocum said, although he was not sure that Mrs. Harmon had stationed herself at the bay window of the boardinghouse. It struck him as something the woman would do. "I'd better get on with my chores. Judge Tunstell wants me to take notices around to some of the townsfolk, telling them about new regulations."

"New?"

"He's trying to get Mayor Grierson to agree to a no-firearms law inside the town limits. There's some argument over it, especially from Alton at the Desert Oasis. He thinks if his customers had to check their six-shooters they wouldn't drink as much. He might be right."

"Yes, John, go on. Do your chores, as you call them." Angela had turned distant. From the corner of his eye, Slocum caught movement behind the boardinghouse curtains. Mrs. Harmon was snooping.

He swung into the saddle and rode slowly away, taking the first street he came to so the buildings blocked Angela's view. He dismounted and went to the corner of the building and looked around it, feeling a bit like the nosy landlady. Slocum was not too surprised to see Angela hurrying along the street heading in the direction of the courthouse. Following her was easy. There weren't many other places in Dry Water she was likely to go. But when she got to the courthouse, Slocum had to scratch his head at her actions.

Rather than go inside, Angela quickly looked around to be sure no one saw her before going to an open window. She crouched underneath and craned her neck in such a way that she could eavesdrop on whatever was being said in the office.

Slocum watched Angela for several minutes. As furtively as she had taken her position under the open window, she left.

Curious, Slocum sauntered to the courthouse and went inside. He counted rooms and saw that the mayor's office was the most likely spot where Angela had been spying. Slocum opened the door and stepped into the room. Huddled together at the mayor's desk, heads so close together they almost touched, sat Judge Tunstell, Roger Williams and Claude Grierson.

"What is it, Mr. Slocum? We're in an important conference."

"Sorry to interrupt you, Judge. I'll talk to you later."

"Close the door behind you as you leave, Slocum," growled Grierson. The mayor looked peeved and the banker was downright livid. Only Tunstell showed any composure.

As Slocum pulled the door shut, the trio continued what had to be an argument. All that Slocum overheard was Grierson saying, ". . . get rid of Bennigan once and for all. Then we'll be living on easy street."

That intrigued him—but not as much as the notion that Angela Enwright had been outside the window, listening to everything.

9

"We don't need you in town anymore, Mr. Slocum." Judge Tunstell leaned back in his chair. He ran his fingers around the edges of a large envelope. "Now that the marshal is back, he can run his own jail. Since your services aren't required there, I want you to take these documents to Sacramento and see them filed with the state supreme court."

"I'm no lawyer," Slocum said. "You'd be better off seeing to it yourself."

"There are too many business matters, uh, and legal ones, here in Dry Water for me to take the documents myself. That you are not a lawyer won't matter. I have associates who will follow through with the actual court appearances needed."

Slocum considered his options. Watching over Calvin Bennigan had been easy enough. Mostly all he had to do was make sure the prisoner was fed, taken to the outhouse now and then, and sit around being bored. The judge's law clerk, Morris, spelled him so he could get food for himself and take a sip or two of whiskey at the saloon. Being on duty at the jailhouse had meant he no longer got to sleep in the fancy bed upstairs at the courthouse. He had found those were the judge's private quarters where he had been nursed back to health.

Slocum tapped his feet. They were in good condition once more. He had recovered fully from his walk back from the fringes of the Mojave Desert. The only thing bad about Marshal Delgado's return was that he had not brought Slocum's saddle with him. Slocum was sorry to lose his gear, but he saw no way to recover it. Even if he could find that particular spot in the maze of canyons spiderwebbed around in the hills, he had to borrow a horse to get there. The judge had made it clear he was no longer interested in loaning horses to be shot out from under Slocum.

"I'll do it," Slocum said. He had come to the conclusion this was his best way out of Dry Water. Let the judge send him to Sacramento. From there he could find another job or somehow get a horse and complete his trip to the coast. As he considered that, Slocum knew that seeing the ocean might be less important than simply staying on the trail north. He wouldn't have a hefty reward to buy himself a string of horses or even much more than enough money to buy himself a mug of beer at some dive, but he would be on the trail. That mattered more than becoming a rich horse breeder.

"Of course you will," Tunstell said dryly. "You work for me. To earn your pay, you'll do it."

"How do I get the papers to Sacramento?"

"I'm certainly not letting you ride. The weekly stagecoach will be through in a few hours. Take it to Pemberton. The railroad does not run to Sacramento, so you must take another stage from there. The entire trip ought to take a week. Ten days at the most." Tunstell took a deep breath and let it out slowly. He stared at the envelope, as if coming to a decision he did not much like. Thrusting it toward Slocum, the judge said, "Get the papers filed."

"All right," Slocum said. The envelope was fat with the documents. He saw how the flap had been sealed with a wax blot imprinted with some fancy crest. The judge was taking no chance Slocum might open the envelope and see what he carried.

While there was a certain amount of curiosity about his chore, Slocum was more interested in using it to get out of Dry Water. Leaving would be something of a regret because he would be leaving Angela Enwright behind, but from all he had seen of her, she would not miss him long. He tucked the large envelope under his arm.

"Wait, Mr. Slocum. Here." The judge tossed him a small, jingling leather bag. "There's enough there for your stage-coach tickets and meals, if you do not eat too high on the hog."

"How much of this do you want back, Judge?"

Tunstell laughed. "You are a piece of work, Slocum. Get out of here. I have too much work to do." With that he turned back to the stacks of paper on his desk.

Slocum dropped the bag of coins into his coat pocket and left. He slowed as he passed the mayor's office. Roger Williams was arguing with Grierson again. All Slocum caught were a few words, but nothing he could put together. He stepped out into the bright California sun. The wind was blowing from the direction of the Mojave, turning the day hotter than ever. As quickly as sweat beaded on his forehead, it evaporated and cooled him.

He considered finding Angela and biding her good-bye, but school was in session. The gossip that would spread through the small town when all those students' tongues got to wagging about how their new teacher had a beau would do more to ruin Angela's reputation than anything she might actually do. Instead, Slocum went to the saloon and knocked back a couple drinks as he waited for the stage to arrive.

When he heard the rattle of chains and creak of leather, Slocum went outside. The saloon doubled as the stage depot. Aboard were two other passengers, both looking exhausted and filthy from their travel. The driver jumped down, then bellowed, "We got ten minutes to change our team. Get likkered up, if that's your pleasure."

"Howdy," Slocum greeted him. "Got a strongbox?" He held out the bundle of papers the judge had given him. Just carrying it from the courthouse had left sweat stains on the paper. Slocum knew if he held on to the documents, they would be filthy by the time he reached Sacramento.

"Surely do. This here envelope's gonna be mighty lonesome in there, though."

"They'll survive," Slocum said, laughing. He saw the driver use a key dangling from a chain around his neck to open the lock. Inside were three small bags, probably silver or gold, and a few letters. The driver stuffed the large envelope in and secured the lock again.

"There you go. You travelin' to Pemberton?"

"And then to Sacramento," Slocum said.

"You're in luck. I'm makin' that run this month. Got itchy feet. I'll see that yer papers are aimed in the right direction. Might have a new strongbox. Might have more—"

Slocum stopped listening to the garrulous driver. The man sat atop the stagecoach all day long, his view of four horses' rears never changing unless he changed to a six-horse team. Slocum didn't mind that the man wanted to hear himself talk some, but it meant nothing to him. To help him along, Slocum worked to exchange teams so they would get on the road sooner.

"You want to ride up here?" the driver asked hopefully. "Could use the company."

"Sorry. Want to ride along like I was paying for a ticket," Slocum said.

"You are," the driver said glumly. He took Slocum's money and waved him into the stagecoach.

Slocum climbed in and found a spot that looked most comfortable. The hard bench seats had been covered with thin pads sheathed in leather, but those were mostly worn through. He settled down as the other two passengers followed him in. One man with a sour look and long black coat sat where he could stare out without saying a word to his fellow passengers. The other man looked to be a peddler. He dropped next to Slocum.

"Good to have some new blood aboard. How are you, this fine day, sir?"

Slocum began to appreciate the driver's offer to ride with him. It took only until the stagecoach reached the edge of Dry Water before the peddler tried to interest him in buying "trinkets for the little lady or perhaps a fine, honed knife with a blade *gar-own-teed* to last a lifetime."

The rolling motion of the coach soon lulled Slocum into a state halfway between alertness and sleep. When the gunshot sounded, Slocum was not sure right away if he was dreaming or it was for real.

Then the stage came to a halt and a strident voice called, "Get on down, driver, or the next shot will be through your worthless head. And get those passengers out here, too."

"We're being robbed!" The peddler was hurriedly going through his pockets, looking for a spot inside the cabin to stash his money. He never found it. The door was yanked open and a rifle was shoved through.

"Out. Now. And thanks for speeding this up."

As the peddler sat and dithered, the road agent made a grab for the greenbacks in the peddler's fist.

"That's mine! I made that selling—"

"You'll be in need of buying, if you don't get out." The outlaw shoved the rifle muzzle into the peddler's belly.

"What? Buy what?"

"A grave, you idiot," grumbled the man. "Get out and let's get this over with." He shoved the peddler out and followed quickly, not even bothering to look at Slocum. Slocum climbed out and looked around. The one outlaw held his rifle on the driver again. Nowhere did Slocum see any other road agents.

"Don't get any funny ideas, mister," the outlaw said, staring hard at Slocum. The man's muddy brown eyes peering over the top of the bandanna pulled up over his nose were alert to any move. "Drop your hogleg. Step away from it. Now give me whatever you got in your pockets."

Slocum reached into his coat pocket and pulled out the leather bag the judge had given him for expenses. The outlaw motioned to him to toss it over. Slocum did.

"What about that fine watch of yours?"

"It was my brother's," Slocum said, not moving to obey. "It's all I have to remember him."

"What's the story?"

"He died during Pickett's Charge."

"Keep your watch," the outlaw said. "I lost my pa at Chancellorsville."

Slocum did not relax but stopped thinking of reaching the man before he could squeeze off a round. The money meant nothing to him. The watch would have cost the road agent his life—if he had tried to steal it.

The outlaw finished cleaning out the pockets of the other two passengers, then said to the driver, "Drag down that strongbox."

The driver grumbled but obeyed. He had the same sense that Slocum did. If he did as he was told, the outlaw wasn't likely to do anything foolish—like gunning them all down.

The strongbox hit the ground hard. Slocum waited for the outlaw to order the driver to open it. The keys were in plain sight on the driver's chest, dangling from a gold chain and glittering in the sunlight.

"Get on back into the stage and vamoose out of here," the road agent ordered.

Slocum looked around again for any sign of others in the man's gang. As far as he could tell, this was a solo robbery.

He climbed into the stage with the other two passengers. The stagecoach rumbled, lurched and started off, pressing Slocum back into the hard bench seat. He let the driver go on for a few hundred yards, then pushed his way past the protesting peddler, opened the door and swung out onto the side of the coach.

"Slow down," Slocum called.

"Ain't doin' it, mister. I want to put distance 'tween me and that varmint."

"The hell," Slocum said. He jumped. Hitting the ground hard, he rolled and came to his feet in a cloud of dust. The heat hammered at him and succeeded in beating out a few more drops of sweat. He swiped at them and turned to look back down the road. The stagecoach rattled on, oblivious to him getting off.

Slocum pulled down his hat to protect his face, lifted his bandanna in an imitation of the road agent's and began walking back to where the holdup had occurred. To his relief the outlaw had left the Colt Navy in the dust where Slocum had dropped it. He took a few minutes to wipe off the six-shooter, cocking it several times to be certain the action was clean and free of grit, then jammed it into his holster.

Studying the ground gave him the direction the outlaw had taken. To Slocum's surprise, the road agent had not bothered shooting off the lock on the strongbox. Not seeing it anywhere, Slocum reckoned the outlaw had taken it with him. That was a puzzle since the box was heavy and didn't contain all that much. The outlaw could not know that, but why hadn't he shot the lock off and left the box after pawing through the contents?

As he walked, Slocum studied the hoofprints. He was not too surprised to see that the front right horseshoe was about ready to come off. The man who had shot at him when he and Angela were on their way to Dry Water was holding up stages now.

A twenty-minute walk in the heat and dust got him to the fork in the road. One direction led to Dry Water. The other wound itself around into the eastern hills where the bank robber had hidden before. Slocum felt as if someone had shoved a bale of cotton into his mouth, but the watering hole farther along the eastern road was closer than Dry Water. More than this, it kept him moving in the direction taken by the road agent.

Running him down on foot looked to be a fool's errand, but Slocum ruefully admitted to himself that he fit the description. He was a damn fool for thinking he could catch the robber without a posse backing him up. Still, Slocum was not inclined to take the time to form a posse. With a bit of luck, which had been elusive of late, he might snare the reward offered by Roger Williams for catching the bank robber and keep it all for himself. With a little less luck, he might get the judge's papers back if the robber dumped the contents of the strongbox and kept only the money. And with a little more luck, Slocum might bring Jackson Kinney's murderer to justice. The best he could figure, the road agent holding up the stagecoach was in cahoots with the bank robber.

By a little after midday Slocum reached the watering hole and drank his fill. He rested in the shade of bushes nearby, drank some more and made a complete circuit of the pond. What he found made him scratch his head. Rather than going for the safety of a hideout in the eastern hills, the rider had left the watering hole and angled toward Dry Water.

The trek across country that made hell look like grassy pastureland took Slocum the better part of the afternoon. He sweat until his clothes clung to his body. Any breeze dried out the cloth and cooled him, but when the wind died he was once more afloat in his own perspiration. Head down, eyes squinted against the bright sunlight, he kept tramping along. He reached Dry Water an hour after sundown. Already the saloon was blaring with bad piano music and the shouts and whistles of increasingly drunk patrons.

Slocum considered going in for a drink or two to wet his whistle. He dunked his head in a water barrel instead. The water turned icy against his skin, and it felt good after the heat he had endured all afternoon. Sitting on the edge of a boardwalk, eyeing the few people moving along the main street, Slocum wondered where he ought to go first.

Judge Tunstell deserved to know his papers had been taken in the robbery and that Slocum had been unable to retrieve them. But Marshal Delgado needed to know that the robber had ridden for town after watering his horse. At this instant the road agent might be bellied up to the bar, swilling pop skull from Alton's special bottle and laughing with the others in the Desert Oasis. Delgado could capture him easily. If he knew who he was.

That the road agent had come to Dry Water in such a circuitous fashion meant he wanted to fool anyone seeing him riding in as to his actual route. Slocum considered the rest of what this implied. The robber could be about anyone who lived in town.

"Anyone who rides a horse with a shoe about to fall off must be known to about everyone in this town." Small-town gossip made a mountain out of any small lump of trouble. Slocum got to his feet. He knew the first place to go.

The blacksmith was still working, his forge a dull orange until the burly man pumped the bellows furiously and got it hotter for the horseshoe he was hammering out.

He looked up as Slocum walked over to him.

"You needin' work done, Slocum? Which of the judge's horses you ridin' now?"

"None of them. You getting ready to shoe a horse?" The way Slocum's feet burned from his most recent hike through the desert, he wished he could have steel shoes put on his boots.

The smithy held up the horseshoe. It was a dull red in the dark. He turned and thrust it into a bucket of water. Slocum watched the steam rise and knew the answer.

"Whose horse is it?" Slocum asked.

"That one yonder. Threw a shoe sometime this afternoon from the look of it."

Slocum changed his mind. The road agent might not be anyone from town. He might have been hightailing it for the hills and only discovered his horse had thrown a shoe. That changed his destination to the nearest farrier.

"You know whose horse it is?"

"Surely do," the smithy said. He hammered a few more times until he was satisfied.

"Right front hoof?"

This stopped the blacksmith. He peered through the gloom at Slocum.

"Now how'd you know that?"

"Good guess."

"Then you probably know it's the mayor's horse."

This came as only a slight surprise to Slocum.

10

Slocum sat in the dark on the boardwalk in front of the bakery, listening to the town around him. Wood creaked as the buildings cooled off. The raucous noises from the saloon told of men trying vainly to forget their day's woes and their body's aches. Mostly, he appreciated the fragrance of cooking bread and other pastries that had soaked into the very walls of the bakery. He closed his eyes and pictured the road agent who had held up the stage. All he remembered exactly were the brown eyes over the bandanna. Nothing of the outlaw's build or other distinguishing marks like scars or hair color had been visible.

It could have been Grierson. There was no doubt that it was the mayor's horse that had thrown a shoe, since Slocum had tracked the road agent's horse to Dry Water. Coincidence was always possible, but Slocum doubted it. Grierson had held up the stage. This was a curious proposition for a politician who could steal from a town's collected taxes. All he needed to do was reach into the pot and pull out a fat handful of greenbacks.

Unless the banker kept the town's revenues all locked up in his vault. Slocum felt his head begin to ache. Williams had claimed his vault was cleaned out, which meant every dime the city had collected in taxes was also missing. That might explain Grierson turning to common thievery. Or it might be something else.

Slocum wondered if his head would explode. He realized breakfast had been his last meal as his belly rumbled in protest. The smell of bread baking added to his hunger. The bakery was closed for business, working on the next day's loaves, but Slocum went around to the back and knocked on the door. It took several minutes before the owner came and peered out.

"Oh, it's you, Slocum. I thought you'd gone to Sacramento for the judge."

"Got back," Slocum said, not wanting to discuss the matter. "I took a whiff of the night air and your bread smelled too good to pass up. Could I get a slice or two? I don't have any money right now, but—"

"Hell, why not? The judge has been good to me. No reason I can't be generous to one of his boys. Here." The baker passed out a loaf of bread that had fallen. Almost flat in the middle but risen on the ends, it was a sight. And it was about the best-tasting bread Slocum had ever eaten.

"Reckon you're back at the marshal's office now?"

"Why?" Slocum slowed stuffing the bread into his mouth so he could speak. Something in the baker's words put him on guard.

"The marshal getting shot up and all."

Slocum said nothing. The baker stared at him.

"You ain't heard? There was another bank robbery this morning. Marshal Delgado tried to stop the varmint and got himself shot."

"How many robbers?"

"Just one. The judge said he thinks it is the same fellow who stuck up the bank before and got away."

"That doesn't make any sense. If he got all the money before, why come back?"

"Can't say. Crooks don't think like me and you, Slocum. I got to get back to work. Don't want to burn the night's work, now, do I?"

"Much obliged," Slocum said, holding up what was left of the loaf. He had eaten all but a fraction of it and it set like stone in his belly. He had eaten too much too fast.

Walking into the middle of the street, he saw a light burning in the jailhouse. There was also a light in the courthouse. If he wanted answers to a passel of questions that had sprung up like weeds in his head, he needed to see Judge Tunstell.

In spite of how his belly ached, he ate until the entire loaf was gone. He brushed the last crumb from his lips when he got to the door of the judge's office.

Tunstell looked up, startled.

"My God, Slocum, what are you doing here?"

"Thought you'd heard by now, Judge. The stagecoach was robbed."

"What!"

"Just outside of town. I had to walk back to Dry Water."

"Son of a bitch!" The judge sagged back in his chair so that his jacket flopped open. Slocum saw the man had a pistol slung in a shoulder rig. Since he had been in Dry Water, Slocum had never seen the judge wear a six-gun.

"You carrying a six-shooter now because of the morning's bank robbery?"

"Not just that," Tunstell said. His eyes narrowed as he peered at Slocum. "For a man who's just blown back into town, you know a considerable amount about what's happened."

"I got something to eat. Heard that the marshal is all shot up."

"It was bad luck on his part. He was going into the bank just as the robber struck. Lead flew all around, Delgado drew and fired. He got hit in the chest. Mighty serious wound, but he's likely to pull through. He's a tough old bird."

Slocum wasn't sure why he asked, "Did the bank robber shoot him?"

"Why do you ask that?"

Slocum held his tongue. The silence forced the judge to answer.

"Can't say. Williams says so, but he was spraying lead all over the place. Put at least three holes in his own ceiling. A teller said the robber never even fired, but Williams says different."

Slocum realized that Williams could be lying to save his own hide. He might have fired at the robber, missed and struck the marshal. An even less charitable thought came to Slocum. Williams might have seen a chance to kill Delgado. Why he would want the marshal dead was something Slocum couldn't answer, but it was definitely an item in the stew pot of Dry Water's dirty dealings.

"Is Bennigan still locked up?"

"He'll stay there until his trial," Tunstell said. "Why do you ask?"

"I had some crazy idea he might have been the robber who escaped after the first holdup."

"Yeah, Mr. Slocum, that's plumb crazy." The judge snorted and pulled his coat down to hide the butt of the pistol protruding from under his arm. "Tell me about the stage robbery."

"Not much to tell. A lone gunman, carried a rifle, took all our money and the strongbox."

"Tell me you still have the papers I gave you." Tunstell was at the point of pleading.

"They were in the strongbox. That was real strange, too. The road agent took the box rather than shooting off the lock and rifling through the contents."

"Mighty odd," Tunstell agreed. "Why carry a heavy box when all he wanted were the valuables in it?"

"I followed him on foot to the watering hole east of the fork going to Pemberton."

"Lose him there?"

Slocum considered his answer. He had seen Grierson and Williams arguing but Tunstell had been with them, so the judge knew the reason for their argument. The trio might be in cahoots. Or they might be double-crossing each other at every turn. Slocum was wondering what was going on in

Dry Water that depended on putting a miner in jail, robbing a stage of legal papers on their way to Sacramento and multiple bank robberies that hardly appeared to be that. Whatever was going on, three men had died and the marshal was laid up with a gunshot to the chest.

"Can't say where he went afterward," Slocum said. Tunstell looked relieved. That was reason enough for Slocum to be glad he had read the situation right.

"We need you more than ever, Mr. Slocum. With the marshal laid up, we have to get a posse together to bring the bank robber to justice."

"I'm not going to wear a badge," Slocum said with enough fire to make the judge sit a little straighter.

"It's your civic duty. The town needs you. I need you. Think of the marshal lying in bed, a gunshot wound in his chest. Think of how Jackson Kinney was cut down during the first robbery."

"And my two horses," Slocum said.

"They were my horses, but you could have been killed. Dry Water needs a deputy right now, Mr. Slocum. You're the best we've got."

"Then you have a piss-poor bunch to choose from."

"There is that," Tunstell agreed. "At least ride with the posse. You are the best tracker in these parts. Delgado said so, and from what you tell me about following the stage robber, you're more determined than anyone else is likely to be."

"I'll do that," Slocum said, regretting it the instant the words slipped from his lips. "But I won't wear a badge."

"I have to wonder about that," Tunstell said, "but I will abide by your decision. In the morning, I'll have someone deputized. You can lead the posse, scout for it, do everything but arrest the owlhoot when you catch up with him. Is that agreeable?"

Slocum nodded.

Slocum groaned when he saw the deputy ride up to get his posse whipped into shape.

"Come on, guys. You got to do like I say. Do it and when we get back, drinks'll be on me!" The barkeep from the Desert Oasis looked forlorn sitting astride his scrawny horse and wearing a deputy's badge that caused his shirt to flop about.

"Do as he says," Slocum snapped. "If we want to find the robber before we die from the heat, we have to work together."

Alton mouthed a silent "thanks" for Slocum's help. The ragtag posse climbed onto their horses. Some were so hungover from the night's drinking that they hardly stayed in the saddle. The rest showed none of the usual eagerness to find a criminal and see him swing.

"What'd the judge promise them?" Slocum asked Alton.

The barkeep looked sheepish and said, "He left that up to me, so I went to Mr. Williams and asked if that reward was still standing. After the second robbery, I thought he might up the ante a mite." Alton shook his head.

"Might be there's no money left in the bank for a reward," Slocum suggested. As they rode from town, Slocum thought on the matter some more. Williams was just not consistent. Slocum wished he could have asked if the money Williams had mentioned for Bennigan's death still stood. For the time being, he thought the miner was as safe in jail as anywhere, although Delgado might disagree.

Slocum had not been able to see what condition the marshal was in nor ask about the guards at the jailhouse. Delgado had lost a prisoner. It might not be too hard to arrange for another one to die.

He shrugged off such speculation. The judge wanted him to scout for the posse. He could do that. As they rode, Slocum kept a sharp eye on the hard ground for signs that the robber had come this way. More than a dozen townspeople had all agreed that he had ridden east. Slocum thought he was heading straight into the hills again.

"If any of you gents spy a saddle and gear, let me know," Slocum shouted. A few in the posse perked up.

"Any reward fer that saddle?"

"My gratitude," Slocum said. "It's my saddle. The varmint we're chasing shot my horse out from under me and I had to leave my gear."

"That there's the third horse you've been on, ain't it, Slocum?" Alton looked closely at Slocum's mount. "I recognize that hunk o' horseflesh. That's the marshal's spare horse."

"Conchita is more of a horse than any of yours," Slocum said, meaning it. Conchita turned her head a bit and fixed him with a large brown eye as if thanking him for the kind words.

"What do you make of that, Mr. Slocum?" asked a man riding on the far side of the posse. He pointed to a scrap of cloth torn off on a thornbush. The cloth matched the shirt pattern and color of the robber's.

"I make it to be our fugitive," Slocum said. He began working harder hunting for a trail. More from instinct than actual spoor, Slocum began working through the desert toward the hills. Only once did he find anything that might have been left by the robber, but in his gut he thought they were on the right trail.

Winding around, they came to a narrow canyon he remembered well. He had ridden this way when his second horse was shot out from under him. Slocum slowed and began looking up at the canyon rim for any sign of a sentry. He had blundered into the camp before, sure that the robber could not know he was coming. Yet he had. That might mean there was a second man he had not seen, one staying out of town and providing an extra measure of safety for the bank robber's escape.

"We ridin' into a trap, Mr. Slocum?" Alton looked pale at the idea. "I don't wanna die."

"You won't. Keep an eye peeled for movement along either rim. That'll mean someone's spotted us and is likely to warn the robber we're on the way."

"Don't see nobody," Alton said.

"Good." Slocum occasionally dropped down to check the tracks. The narrow canyon did not allow a rider to deviate from the path. He wanted to study the imprints of the horse-shoes more closely. The horse they tracked had all four shoes firmly affixed.

Swinging back into the saddle when they emerged from the narrow canyon, Slocum silently pointed. The posse fanned out in a single line stretching from one side of the valley to the other.

"We can't sweep all the way through here, Mr. Slocum," Alton said. "The valley gits a whole lot wider. The men'll be hundred yards or more apart."

"Won't have to spread out that much," Slocum said. He took a deep whiff of the air. "That robber surely does eat well. He was cooking venison before."

"Stew?" Alton looked around nervously. "That what I'm smellin'?"

Slocum nudged his heels to Conchita's flanks and rocketed forward, letting the rest trail behind. He felt the robber slipping away again. He slowed only when he reached the spot where he had first encountered the robber—and his accurate rifle fire. In the same fire pit as before a kettle bubbled and boiled. The savory stew had been left just as the venison had.

"Spread out, men," Slocum called. "Search the entire area. Be damned careful, though. You're likely to be ambushed."

Slocum hit the ground and looked around before the men returned and messed up the campsite. A smile came to his lips. He had been right. There had been two men here. One had ridden in from the west—that would be the robber. The other had come from the south.

"Alton!" Slocum bellowed. "You know this country?"

"A little, Slocum."

"If we ride south, where's that take us?"

"Well, lemme think. I seem to recollect a trail meandering around that ends up somewhere south of town."

"You can ride from Dry Water directly here?"

"Well, it's not too direct. A long trail that winds through the hills."

"Nobody'd see you if you came that way?"

"Not likely since all the miners have moved on. The countryside down that way used to be filthy with mines and miners."

"Like Cal Bennigan," Slocum said. He still couldn't fit everything together so it made any sense, but he was figuring out more of the entire picture. Or at least looking at new pieces.

"We don't see nobody, Slocum," called a man in the posse. Three others reported back quickly enough. The robber and his accomplice had faded away before they could enjoy their meal of stew.

Slocum poked about in the ashes of the fire and found something wrapped in paper. He opened it up. Bread. He tore off a chunk and chewed on it. He remembered the taste well. This had come from the bakery in Dry Water.

"Help yourselves to the stew, men," Slocum said, munching on the bread as he walked around. "I don't know what else we're likely to find."

"You mean he done gave us the slip?"

Slocum looked at the barkeep. Alton was hopeful that was the case. Slocum decided his eagerness came more from a desire to return to Dry Water than it did from relief that the robber had gotten away. Everyone in the posse had either been browbeaten into coming along or had been prodded by greed and a big reward.

As the men sat and ate, Slocum circled the camp, then climbed into rocks above the campsite. From here a man had a clear view to knock any approaching rider out of the saddle. Slocum held out his arm and pointed his finger. The robber had hit what he aimed at before. If he had wanted to kill Slocum, it would have been an easy shot. Instead, he had killed his horse. That left Slocum alive and yet afforded the robber quick escape.

"He's not much of a killer, then," Slocum said. That didn't fit with the stories of the second bank robbery that left Marshal Delgado shot up. Or Jackson Kinney getting gunned down during the first robbery.

And it did not answer how the suspect in the first robbery had been killed in the jail cell. Too many pieces, not enough clarity.

Slocum knelt and picked up a spent shell casing. The bright brass cartridge had been fired recently. The wind and sand had not yet dulled its gleam.

"This is the one that killed my horse," Slocum said softly. He climbed higher into the rocks and found a level area. He pounced on the strongbox like a vulture swooping down on a fresh carcass. Pulling back the lid, he looked inside. It came as no surprise that it was empty.

Slocum closed the lid and sat on the box, thinking hard. It made no sense that the bank robber and the stagecoach robber were one and the same, yet finding the strongbox here put that to the test. How else could the strongbox have gotten here?

"Two of them," Slocum said to himself. "I'm looking for two owlhoots."

11

Alton looked more confident and relaxed in his usual position behind the bar. The Desert Oasis was crammed to the walls tonight. Slocum nursed a drink and studied the men in the room. The thought came that one of them might be the bank robber or his partner. The notion that two men were out there working to rob the town bank gave Slocum pause, though.

If Williams was telling the truth about the first robbery being as much as ten thousand dollars, why had the robber stuck around? There could be nothing left in the bank vault. Yet the robber had made a second robbery attempt. This one had resulted in Delgado getting shot, but the attempt itself was what intrigued Slocum. It was as if there was something still in the bank other than money that the robber wanted.

The robber and his partner were as mysterious as they were dangerous. Were both of them in the saloon tonight? Slocum knew it would be smart if they were. The only reason he could think for the robber to remain was that he lived in Dry Water. Even as this thought crossed his mind, he found himself doubting it. The two dead robbers had not been locals. Why should the third be? And maybe the fourth?

Slocum knocked back his whiskey and let it burn all the

way down to his belly. It took away his aches and pains and made him feel downright sociable.

"You want another, Slocum?"

"Hit me," Slocum told the barkeep. Alton poured, running the amber liquid right to the rim.

"Just for you," Alton said.

"You think we could get a new posse to go out again?" Slocum asked. The bartender turned pale at the thought.

"Could, but why bother?" Alton took a quick pull on the bottle to get a little Dutch courage. "We run that varmint off. Didn't we?"

"We didn't find him, and the contents of the strongbox from the stage were gone."

"Couldn't be anything too important," the barkeep declared. "We run him off, Slocum. I know it."

"Could be," Slocum allowed, seeing how uncomfortable Alton was with the idea of being a deputy again on another ride into the countryside. "Then, there's plenty of crooked dealings here in town."

"You don't have to live here long to know that, do you?" Alton chuckled and leaned forward to talk to Slocum in a conspiratorial whisper. "I declare that mayor of ours is as crooked as a dog's hind leg."

"The mayor? I thought you meant Williams. Aren't the two of them in cahoots?"

"Sure thing, they are. I suspect Judge Tunstell is throwed in with 'em, too."

"Doing what?"

"Can't rightly say, but it must be important. There's not a living soul in Dry Water that's not seen the three of them arguing. If anybody gets too close, they stop and pretend to be buddies."

"Could be something to do with the miner. What do you think of him?"

"Cal? What I think of him is that he don't pay off what he owes me too often. No skin off my nose havin' him in the hoosegow."

"He's not rich?"

"Whatever gave you that idea, Slocum? He gets by. That's about it. That claim of his yields enough gold to keep him from starving, but barely."

This was about what Slocum had figured. Bennigan hardly looked to be living in the lap of luxury. If it wasn't the man's mine that Williams and the rest wanted, what was it?

"Slocum! Hey, Slocum, the judge wants to see you. Right now."

Slocum looked at the man in the doorway and waved him over. Morris, the judge's clerk, came quickly on bowed legs.

"You tell him. I was here?"

"Naw, he knew. He's kinda pissed that you didn't report straight to him when the posse got back."

"Why don't you keep my place for me?" Slocum said, slapping the man on the back. "Alton'll take good care of you."

Slocum left the smoking saloon and stepped into the crisp desert air. He sucked in a deep breath and knew he could no longer put off reporting to Judge Tunstell everything that had happened. Going to the courthouse felt like climbing the steps to the gallows. Slocum wondered why he felt this way when he had done nothing wrong.

He just hadn't found out anything worthwhile.

"Get on in here, Slocum. Shut the door," the judge bellowed. The thin-as-a-rail man impatiently waited for Slocum.

"What can I do for you, Judge?"

"Dammit, man, you know. Did you get the papers back?"

"I found the strongbox in the robber's camp . . . but it was empty." Slocum shook his head.

"No hope of tracking that son of a bitch?"

"Nope."

The judge sank down into his chair, grumbling to himself. He finally straightened and leaned forward.

"If I thought for an instant you were double-dealing me, Slocum—"

"What would you do?" Slocum was at the end of his rope. He was not the judge's lackey to be bullied.

"You wouldn't want to know."

"I've got places to go, Judge," Slocum said, standing.

"Shut up and sit down. I haven't dismissed you."

Slocum stared at the man. The judge had been unfailingly formal and polite before. He was being eaten alive by something now, and it had to do with the papers that had been lost in the robbery.

"What were the papers, Judge? What made them so all-fired important?"

"I'm not sure telling you would serve a purpose." The judge stared at Slocum, then said tiredly, "That's wrong. It will serve a purpose. It'll keep you around. Don't walk out on me yet. Please, Mr. Slocum."

Slocum sat down and waited for Tunstell to get his thoughts in order. It took longer than it should have for a man as clever with words as the judge.

"The papers were the original documents for Bennigan's mine. We're trying to foreclose on him and have to get legal approval from Sacramento."

"That's mighty odd," Slocum said. "This is all within your bailiwick."

"Normally. Not this time. I want everything to be absolutely correct. Now that the papers are lost, I have to find some other way of removing Bennigan."

"Buy him out."

"We've tried. He's got this idea that the mother lode is just a few more inches away, and if he keeps working his claim, he will find it eventually." Tunstell shook his head. "There's no mother lode. Not a one of the other mines turned up even a fraction of the gold Bennigan has already taken from his hole in the ground."

"Then why do you want it?"

"We have our reasons."

"We? You, Williams and Grierson?"

"I represent a group interested in Bennigan's property for reasons other than mining. Leave it at that, Mr. Slocum."

"So the lost papers mean you can't boot him off his property?"

"I need to get copies of the papers. I've wired for them to be prepared and sent, but it will take some time. If Bennigan would cooperate, we could construct the papers here."

"He's no fool. He knows he'll be left out in the cold."

"Do you know who the robber is, Mr. Slocum?"

"I thought it might be somebody local but that doesn't make a whole lot of sense." Slocum wondered if he should tell Tunstell that he suspected the stagecoach robber was none other than the mayor. Whatever deal the banker, mayor and judge had, they were actively trying to screw each other out of it for their own gain. There seemed no decent reason to voice his suspicions. Either Tunstell knew his partner was working against him or he at least suspected.

"Go tell whoever's watching Bennigan to let him go."

"You're not keeping him under lock and key?" This surprised Slocum.

"Since the papers are lost, it's going to be a week or more before I can get official copies. No need putting the town to the expense of guarding Bennigan."

"You'll have to pry him loose from his claim all over again, eviction or not from the capital."

"I'm aware of that. I keep thinking there might be some other way of dealing with Mr. Bennigan."

Slocum knew what way Williams wanted him dealt with. He started to ask if Tunstell had the same fatal end in mind and then shelved that, too. Again, if Tunstell didn't know the caliber of his partners, he was stupider than Slocum gave him credit for being.

Slocum studied Tunstell for a moment. Whatever scheme the judge had in mind, he knew he was part of it.

"The sooner he's sprung from jail, the better he'll like it."

"Go on, Mr. Slocum. Tend to it. I doubt the late hour will

matter to him." Tunstell turned back to the stacks of paper on his desk, slowly thumbing through a sheaf. He paid no further attention, so Slocum left.

Again the sharp night air cut at his lungs, invigorating him. He walked quickly to the jailhouse and went inside. Tunstell's law clerk was standing watch. If sleeping with his head on his crossed arms could be called watching. Slocum didn't bother waking Morris. After all, he had brought the message from the judge earlier. That probably tired him out. He suspected Tunstell worked him all day and then forced him to stand guard at night.

Taking the keys off the peg on the wall, Slocum opened the door into the cell block. Calvin Bennigan lay with his back to the cell door. He came awake when Slocum rattled the keys and fumbled a mite getting the cell door open.

"You can go," Slocum announced.

"Wha? What's going on? Why you lettin' me go?" Bennigan looked around, eyes wide with fear.

"Nobody's going to gun you down for trying to escape," Slocum said. "If you want, I'll ride with you back to your claim."

"You're 'bout the only one of these owlhoots I trust. Am I wrong?"

"No, you're not," Slocum said tiredly. He had ridden a goodly distance today and his eyelids were threatening to fall shut at any instant.

"I can go? No shit?"

"No shit," Slocum said.

Bennigan pushed past, then hesitated. He eyed Slocum suspiciously. "You don't want nuthin' from me?"

"I'd like an answer to a question, but you don't have to give it to me unless you want to."

"What's the question?"

"Why do the Dry Water city fathers want your mine so bad? By all accounts, it's not making you rich. There aren't any big claims out there. Fact is, you're killing yourself to eke out a living."

"Gold," Bennigan said, his eyes glowing as brightly as the metal itself. "It's always about gold. Soon as I pump out the lower level of the mine, I'm sure I'm gonna hit it big."

"Your mine's flooded?"

"Happens," Bennigan said. "But I got a rebuilt pump, and I know there's a ton of gold waitin' there for me."

"Good luck getting to it," Slocum said.

Bennigan still hesitated, then edged away as if he thought Slocum might try to shoot him in the back. He got to the door leading to the office, turned and bolted. Slocum followed. The law clerk moaned softly in his sleep. Slocum couldn't tell if it was a nightmare or a good dream. He scribbled a quick note for Morris, telling him to report to the judge and verify that it was all right to release Bennigan.

This time the air did not revive him the way it had before. Slocum knew he was reaching the end of his rope. He wasn't bunked down in the courthouse anymore, not since he got himself patched up. He had been sleeping in the stables. That was as good a place to go curl up as any. In the morning he could see Marshal Delgado and find how he was doing. With a little dickering, he might be able to buy Conchita from him. Slocum marveled at how such a broke-down-looking horse could be so strong and steady.

"Delgado," he mumbled to himself. "Ought to see him." A slow smile came to his lips. There was someone else he ought to see. If he waited until morning, he wouldn't have a chance since she would be in the schoolhouse with a horde of urchins screaming for her attention.

Slocum veered from going to the stables and headed for Mrs. Harmon's boardinghouse. As he neared, Slocum saw furtive movement under Angela's window. His six-shooter slid easily to his hand. Step by cautious step he advanced to see who might be peeking into Angela's room. When he got close enough, he saw that he had it all wrong. Someone wasn't looking in, someone was climbing out.

From the rustle of skirts, he knew it had to be Angela escaping Mrs. Harmon's Argus-eyed watchfulness. He wouldn't put it past the old woman to sleep in the front room with one eye propped open.

Slocum holstered his six-gun and walked slowly in the shadows on the opposite side of the street from Angela. The woman worked her way toward the courthouse, moving as stealthily as an Indian. He was not too surprised to see the woman go to the mayor's office window. She stood and peered in, then ducked back.

Stride lengthening, Slocum went to her but she had already moved on. He thought he knew where. Not slowing, he circled the courthouse and found her trying to find a spot to get through the bushes under Judge Tunstell's window. Unlike the mayor, the judge had his window open. Perfect for eavesdropping.

"Nice night, isn't it?" Slocum said softly. Angela jumped as if he had stuck her with a pin.

He also saw the way her hand moved to the folds of her skirt and remained there, even when she saw who had spoken.

"You scared me, John. Sneaking up on a body is not good. I do declare." She fanned herself with her left hand. Her right never budged from her side and the thick folds of cloth in her skirt.

"You don't have to shoot me," Slocum said.

"Whatever are you saying?"

He moved faster than she could, grabbing her wrist and pulling her hand into sight. A derringer gleamed silver and deadly in the pale moonlight. She struggled for a moment, then relaxed.

"A girl's got to protect herself," she said. "Even in a peaceable town like Dry Water."

"Not so peaceful lately," Slocum said. "Two bank robberies, a robber killed in the jail and another shot dead while trying to rob the bank, a man murdered in the street, a stagecoach robbery. Not peaceful at all."

"It's a good thing you came along, then," she said, moving closer to him. She pressed so closely Slocum could catch a whiff of her perfume. Her chestnut hair caught moonbeams and turned them into a glory of colors. She tipped her face up to his and half closed her eyes. The way her lips parted left nothing to the imagination.

Slocum kissed her. She crushed herself to him. He felt her tender breasts mashed between them and her entire body quivering with need.

He broke off the kiss and looked up.

"The judge isn't in his office. He's probably over at the first office you tried to eavesdrop on."

"John, I never—"

"You did." He kept hold of her wrist with the derringer still clasped in her hand and pulled her away from the courthouse until they were hidden behind a woodpile. "What did you expect to overhear?"

"I thought I heard something moving in the bushes. A varmint, maybe."

Slocum said nothing. It was a feeble excuse when they both knew what she had intended. He was not sure he wanted a real explanation as much as for her not to lie.

"Come along. You haven't seen it yet."

"Where are we going?" Slocum found the grip reversed. She held his wrist now and pulled him along behind her like a balky child.

"I haven't shown you my schoolroom."

"Saw the inside of one once."

"That's what I thought," Angela said. "You need some more instructing."

"Do I, now?" Slocum laughed and let her guide him up the steps and into the darkened classroom.

"My desk," she said breathlessly. Slocum thought she had run short of air as she headed briskly up the last few steps, but he saw how wrong he was as she hurried to the front of the classroom and was bathed in the moonlight angling through a window.

The silvery light caught bare skin. As she walked, Angela stripped off her blouse and tossed it aside. Her breasts swung gently as she moved. The nipples were dark, almost bloodred in the light. She unfastened her skirt and stepped out of it, naked except for her high-button shoes. Angela turned toward him and perched on the edge of her desk. Her legs separated a little, casting shadows in the most beguiling places.

The chestnut thatch between her legs looked dark and inviting, but not as inviting as the woman's lips. She pouted just a little, then licked her lips. She left liquid silver behind as her tongue vanished back into her mouth. But Slocum found himself staring at her breasts as she cupped them in her hands.

Bouncing gently, she stroked from base to tip, then tweaked hard. She groaned.

"I want you doing this, John. I want to feel your mouth all over my breasts. I want to feel more here." Her right hand slipped slowly from her breast down across her belly to the tangled forest hiding her nether lips. She began stroking slowly, deliberately. Every stroke across those gates to her sex caused Slocum to get a bit harder.

He discarded his gun belt and started unbuttoning his jeans. Walking was more difficult for him as the jeans slid down his legs and hobbled him, but his erection was freed and bucking like a bronco.

Angela's bright eyes fixed on that massive staff. She reached out and took him in hand. Tightening her grip just a little encouraged him to step forward and push his hands into her breasts. The soft, warm flesh flowed under his questing fingers until he caught both nips and began squeezing down on them.

This produced an instant response in the woman. The hand circling his manhood tightened. And she began running her finger in and out of herself, moaning louder now.

"What lesson does the teacher want to give today?" Slocum asked.

"I'll answer any questions you might have."

"How tight are you?" Slocum let her guide him to where her finger had been stroking just seconds before. Angela hopped up on the desk, sending papers cascading to the floor. She leaned back on her elbows and hiked her feet to the edge of the desk. Her knees parted, giving him full access to her most intimate region.

He slid forward an inch more. Both of them trembled in reaction.

"More, John, I need more. Fill me up!"

He stroked over her breasts, down between them, then around her body and under until he could grab a double handful of ass flesh. He lifted and scooted her toward him.

As she moved, so did Slocum. He sank deeper into her heated, moist interior. A lewd squishing sound filled the empty schoolroom. Slocum gripped her behind even tighter and began stroking. Every thrust took him just a little deeper into her smooth, wet, hot core.

She began thrashing about, impaled on his fleshy spike. Her legs curled up until her knees were almost pressing into her chest. Slocum had to change his grip. He slipped his hands around and went up to where he could hold her by the shoulders. This kept her from sliding away with his increasingly furious stroking.

Together they moaned and strained. Slocum pulled her down powerfully around him and she began rotating her hips to stir him around in her interior. Before Slocum realized it, he felt the white-hot tide rising within him. When Angela gasped and tightened around him, this was as much as he could take. He shot his load.

For what seemed an eternity they were locked together in mutual pleasure, and then they slipped apart. Slocum stood at the edge of the desk, staring down at the naked woman. Moonlight turned her into something angelic. The skin was whiter than marble, but no stone had ever been so warm and enticing. Slocum reached down and pressed a hand into her breasts. Angela put her hand on top of his to keep it there.

Her eyelids flickered open and a smile came to her lips.

"You've learned everything I can teach you," she said. "You get an A plus."

"I don't know," Slocum said. "I might have to be kept after school."

"But you weren't bad," Angela replied.

"Remedial lessons," Slocum said. "I may need some remedial lessons."

Angela was the one to give them to him.

12

"You look like hell, Mr. Slocum. Did you sleep poorly?" Judge Tunstell peered closely at Slocum as he sank into a chair that felt as if it were devouring him.

"I got used to the bed upstairs in your spare room," Slocum said. "Sleeping on a hard place is wearing on me." Slocum didn't bother telling the judge that he and Angela had made love long into the night and the hard surface he had slept on was the schoolmarm's desk. He had barely awakened in time to get out before dawn. School would now be in session. Slocum had to wonder how Angela looked.

Probably just fine. But she would have to rearrange her desk after they had made love, scattering papers to the four winds.

"I'm not in the habit of renting out space," the judge said.

"Wasn't asking. I can find a place to sleep over in the livery. Don't mind sleeping surrounded by horses."

"You're still riding the marshal's spare?"

"Conchita's a mighty fine pony," Slocum said. "She doesn't look it, but she's about the best horse in this town."

"My black stallion would disagree," the judge said, chuckling now. "Be that as it may, I have a new chore for you."

Slocum guessed what it would be before the judge spoke again.

"I want you to get Cal Bennigan to sell his place. I don't care if he gives it over to the bank, or me, or even Mayor Grierson. It is proving more difficult to evict him legally than I had thought."

"Are you considering illegal means?" Slocum thought the time he had brought Bennigan in to the jail had been over the boundaries of the law, but he said nothing about that.

"Don't be absurd. I would never do that. This is all above-board. Legal, down to the last dotted i and crossed t."

"Why do you want me to go then?"

"I . . . I think you might have a rapport with him that others in Dry Water lack."

Slocum saw now why Tunstell had insisted that he be the one to free Bennigan from jail the night before. The miner might think of him as an ally and listen when he said to sell the claim. Slocum had no intention of playing on whatever bond there might have been, but he was interested to see how the judge plotted and planned. The man was about as devious as they came.

"You can offer him anything to get him off his claim," Tunstell went on.

"Anything? That's a mighty high number."

"Let me rephrase that. Offer him up to a thousand dollars. However much less he sells for, well, you earn the difference as a bonus for your hard work."

Slocum chewed that over for a minute.

"So, if he sells for eight hundred, I get two hundred?"

"Or the other way around. If Mr. Bennigan sells for two hundred, you retain the balance."

"That's mighty generous," Slocum said. "Or it might mean I end up with squat."

"It all depends on how persuasive you are, Mr. Slocum," Tunstell said dryly. "I cannot get copies of the deeds and other papers I need to foreclose and evict him for at least a month."

"What's the hurry? Take an extra month."

"It is more complex than that, Mr. Slocum. Time has value. I need to act quickly in this matter."

Slocum wondered what that matter might be. What was another month to a man like Tunstell? He controlled the courts. He more or less controlled Marshal Delgado. It appeared that Grierson and Williams were always at each other's throat. That meant Tunstell came in as peacemaker or even swooped in to pick up the pieces the two left because of their bickering. However it was cut, the judge came out on top.

"Time," Slocum muttered. "Time."

Before Tunstell could reply, the office door swung open. Slocum turned, his hand going to his Colt Navy. He disliked sitting with his back to a door, but he had thought it was safe enough in the judge's office. Seeing the banker did not cause him to relax. He left his fingers lightly curled around the ebony butt of his six-shooter, just in case.

"What's the meaning of you bursting in like this, Roger? You didn't even knock!" The judge was furious. Slocum was enough of a poker player to know real from feigned outrage. The judge was angry. Slocum saw that he had also slipped his hand under his coat and undoubtedly clutched at the butt of the six-gun he had in his shoulder rig.

"You sending this yahoo out to Bennigan's claim?" Williams turned to Slocum. "I offered you money before to do the job. You didn't take it, did you, Slocum?" Williams was so mad he was close to stuttering. "I'll give you five hundred. Is that enough to take care of the problem once and for all?"

"Be quiet, Roger," snapped Judge Tunstell. "If I hear you offering blood money and anything happens to Bennigan, I might be inclined to toss you in the hoosegow for conspiracy to commit a crime."

"You'd be responsible, too, dammit," Williams said. "We have to settle this matter."

"What matter is that?" Slocum asked, hoping the banker would answer.

"Be quiet, dammit," flared the judge. "I'm sending Mr. Slocum on his way with incentive enough. If you try to pay for a man's death, I'll see you in jail—next to the man who collects that blood money." Tunstell scowled at Slocum.

"I'd better get on the trail," Slocum said. He stood but kept his hand near his pistol. Williams had a six-gun tucked into the waistband of his pants, but from the bulges under his arms, he might have two more smaller pistols slung there. Slocum couldn't help wondering how threatened Tunstell and Williams were. Neither had carried pistols before the bank robbery. Now, after the second attempt, both did.

As he pushed past Williams, the banker clutched at his arm and whispered, "The offer stands, Slocum. To hell with what Tunstell says. The offer stands!"

Slocum said nothing as he pulled free and kept walking. The hair on the back of his neck rose. He halfway expected Williams to send a heavy hunk of lead into his spine. But he got out the front doors of the courthouse and into the warm desert morning without getting shot. How much longer he could make that claim was something Slocum wondered about.

As he rode Conchita from town, he passed the schoolhouse. Angela stood in the doorway ringing a big brass bell to call the children to class. She looked mighty fine. He wondered how many of the students thought so. The woman waved, and Slocum tipped his hat in reply. Then he was out of town and riding south toward the Holey Mine.

By the time Slocum reached the mine, he was not certain he wanted to exchange words with Bennigan. He certainly did not want to exchange gunfire.

"Hello!" he called. Slocum remained astride Conchita and waited for some movement either near the shack or from the mine. He knew how touchy miners got about unexpected visitors. What was worse, he knew that Bennigan would be expecting someone to call on him. The miner wasn't above answering with a shotgun blast.

"That you, Slocum?"

"It's me. Reckon you know why I'm here and who sent me."

"You gonna gun me down?"

"I won't do that. Williams offered a passel of money for

your head, but I won't do it. Don't much like bankers."
Slocum smiled ruefully. "Certainly don't much like Roger
Williams."

"Ain't nobody in town what does," Bennigan said. The
man came up, seemingly from the middle of a stretch of
level ground. He pushed aside a board that had been covered
with rocks to camouflage his hiding place.

"You spend the night there?"

"Naw, slept in my own bed. Didn't figger even you'd be out
here till about now." Bennigan used the butt of his rifle as a
lever to pull himself out of the hole where he had been hiding.
Once he got to the ground, he swung the rifle back around in
Slocum's direction. Slocum didn't budge an inch. He could
have gunned down the miner at any time, if he had wanted.

"Let me get the questions the judge wants me to ask out
of the way. You want to sell this place?"

"Naw, the Holey is all I got. And there's plenty of gold in
it. I jist know it deep in my gut."

"I'm not a geologist, but there can't be that much around
here. Rocks all look wrong. Nobody else has found gold
worth mentioning."

"I can't say I have, either," Bennigan said. "But it's something I done all by my lonesome. I found it. And I'm seein' it
through. I might starve to death, but I'll do it diggin' in *my*
mine."

Slocum understood. Calvin Bennigan had spent his life fail-
ing. This was his first and maybe only chance to be a success.

"I can offer a fair price for the land. More than fair, if you
want my honest opinion."

"You struck me as a straight shooter, Slocum. Don't even
tell me what you're offerin'. It'd be fair, I know. I won't feel
bad if I don't know."

"Mind if I get down? Poor old Conchita is starting to
shake a mite."

"That there's the marshal's horse, ain't it?"

"I'm borrowing it while he's recuperating."

"Sad thing, that robbery. I heard it all."

"From the jailhouse?"

"I looked out the window as the varmint was ridin' off." Bennigan frowned. "Ya know, Slocum. It never occurred to me before. The shots that cut down the marshal came after the robber was in the saddle."

"Do tell."

"Might have been more 'n one of 'em. They breed like flies. Bank robbers, I mean."

"Bankers, too," Slocum said. This brought a laugh from the miner.

"Come on up, Slocum. I got a pint. We kin each have a little nip."

"Don't mind if I do." Slocum led Conchita to a water barrel and let the horse drink while he went into the small shack. Bennigan already had his bottle out. Slocum saw a drop of whiskey on the miner's lower lip, telling him that Bennigan had already taken a snort. He poured a little into a tin cup and scooted it across to Slocum.

Slocum sat and lifted the tin cup in a silent toast to the miner. The whiskey burned all the way down.

"What should I tell Judge Tunstell?"

"Tell him whatever you want, Slocum. I ain't sellin' out."

"Is there anything else here the judge might want to buy? He's bound and determined to throw you off your property. He's got a request in for duplicate papers to file so you'll lose all this for not paying your taxes."

"I paid. That's why he has to forge all them other papers."

Slocum knew that the miner was on shaky ground. When a man like Tunstell got down to work, he could find a dozen legal reasons to steal property.

"He'll get the Holey Mine, come hell or high water. Fact is, he's in a real hurry. Is there anything here that'll happen within a week or two that he might want to cash in on?"

"Nope, nuthin'," Bennigan said. He took another pull on the whiskey. "If you want, come on into the mine. I'll show you where I'm workin'. You said 'nuff to make me think you know a bit about minin'."

"I'd appreciate it." Slocum was curious to see if he might learn the reason why the judge and his partners were so keen on getting Bennigan off this claim.

"Come on up. I got to do some work on my pump. Damn lower level's flooded. Got worse while I was locked up."

They went to the mouth of the mine. Slocum took a deep whiff. The fetid odor told of dead animals inside. He pulled his hat down squarely around his ears to protect his head from the low ceiling, ducked and followed Bennigan inside. The miner silently handed him a carbide lamp, then made his way deeper into the hillside.

As he walked along, not quite bent over but aware of his hat brushing the ceiling, Slocum studied how Bennigan had put in his support beams. Overhead they looked secure, but the side timbers were bowed and ready to collapse. This didn't make him feel any safer following the miner deeper into his mine.

"There the devil is," Bennigan said.

Slocum held up his carbide lantern and saw a pump sitting on the edge of a pit. Leaning out so he could look down, he saw dark water moving sluggishly below.

"How far down have you dug?"

"Only two levels. Both of 'em below this are flooded."

"Is it worth pumping them out?"

Bennigan snorted in contempt. "Damn right it is. No tellin' how much gold's down there."

Slocum did what he could to study the wall of the shaft leading down to the flooded lower levels. The rock looked exactly like the rock along the shaft reaching this point. Bennigan could work until his fingers wore down to nubbins and never get enough gold out of this mine to be worthwhile.

"You mind holdin' on to this here wrench whilst I whale away at the pump? That's all it'll take to get it runnin' again."

Slocum gripped the wrench to hold a shaft into position. Bennigan swung hard and slammed a sledgehammer into the end of the axle. A second swing almost seated the axle. As he reared back for a third swing, he lost his balance and tumbled into the pit. Slocum dropped the wrench and held out the carbide lantern as he heard a splash below. Shining his light around, he caught sight of Bennigan floundering in the water.

"How deep is it?" Slocum called.

"Waist deep. I kin stand, but there's a powerful current 'gainst my legs."

Slocum saw Bennigan disappear from sight. Even a sluggishly flowing stream could take a man off his feet. The power of moving water was nothing to underrate.

"Bennigan!"

Slocum heard the miner thrashing about below but knew he had no chance to escape unless he got help in a hurry. Looking around, Slocum saw a couple coils of rope. He lashed one around the sturdiest of the supports and tied the other end around his waist. He similarly tied the other coil around a different support, then began lowering himself into the pit. The deeper he went, the more obvious it was that Bennigan had broken through the channel of an underground river.

"Hang on, old-timer. I'll be there in a couple seconds."

Slocum splashed about in the water, glad he had secured the rope around his waist. He fought the flow, which proved stronger than he had expected.

"Here, catch!" Slocum tossed the other rope to Bennigan. "Tie it around your waist. You can use it to get out of the pit."

"Easier said 'n done." Bennigan swore a blue streak until he finally secured it about himself. Hand over hand he worked himself back to where Slocum could grab him and pull him upright.

"Can you get up or do you need me to pull you up?"

"I kin do it. Hell, Slocum, I ain't a baby." Bennigan gripped the rope, pulled himself up a few feet and then got his feet braced against the wall. He made slow progress to the lip of the pit and then vanished.

Slocum began working his way up in the same fashion, hand over hand, feet slipping and sliding against the smooth rock. But he saw the mouth of the pit grow larger as he climbed higher. Then he realized something was wrong. The rope seemed to be getting longer.

"Bennigan, my rope's breaking!"

No answer from above.

Slocum tried to climb faster, but the sharp edge of the pit cut through his old rope. He was close enough to see strand after strand pop and snap until only half the rope remained. He grabbed for the rim of the pit as the rest of the rope broke free.

He grabbed and missed.

Slocum plunged downward into the pit and the raging underground river.

13

Slocum splashed around in the water, struggling to keep from being swept deeper into the tunnel. Bennigan had said he had a second, lower gallery. If Slocum was swept to a hole over that gallery, he would be pulled under and drowned.

He fought for his balance and got to his feet. His boots slipped on the slick rock as the water tried to knock him over like a ten pin. Fingers grasping, he caught an outjut of rock and held on until his hands were running with blood. He gritted his teeth and pulled hard, forcing himself to stay under the mouth of the pit.

Looking up, all he saw was the blue-white light cast by the carbide lantern he had left beside the pit. No shadows of Bennigan moving about, and not even a hint that the rope that had given way was still in place. His mind jumped to wild schemes. If he could jump high enough, he could catch the severed rope and pull himself up. But the edge of the pit was more than ten feet above his head. Even if he could jump that far, the rope would be useless. It had cut at the sharp edge of the pit. And if he could jump that high, he could not even hope to hang on to the rocky lip. It had severed a rope. It would cut through his already lacerated fingers.

"Bennigan!"

All he heard was the rush of water around him. Grimly determined, Slocum tried to edge his way up the rocky walls by forcing his feet against one side and his back against the other. The water made the rock too slippery to climb like this. He fell back heavily.

"You down there, Slocum? What happened?"

"The rope broke!"

Another rope came snaking out into sight and splashed down only inches from him. Slocum wrapped it around his middle and tied it the best he could.

"I can't pull myself out. You need to help. Watch out for the edge of the hole. It's like a knife."

Slocum grunted as the rope tightened under his arms, and he was jerked a foot above the water. Bit by bit, he was painfully pulled aloft until he could reach out and grab the edge of the pump. Using this, he dragged himself free and flopped on the dirty mine floor. It took him several seconds to get his breath back.

"Where the hell did you go?"

"Got to the top. Thought I heard somebody outside, so I went to take a look. Was only a racoon rootin' around, huntin' fer food. When I hied on back, I heard you cryin' down there."

"I damned near drowned," Slocum said.

"Lucky that the 'coon waddled off so I could git on back to you, wasn't it?"

Slocum started to tell Bennigan what he thought of a food-stealing racoon and a man who tended that before making sure his rescuer was safe, but he held his tongue. He sat and wiped the water off the best he could, but he was getting a chill.

"Let me outside," he said. Drying off would take only minutes in the hot desert sun. The air was like a sponge, and the hot wind blowing from the direction of the Mojave soon dried his clothing to his body. His boots had to have the water dumped out, but otherwise Slocum was no worse for the dunking. If anything, he was a sight cleaner than when he had entered the mine.

"You don't think I tried to kill you, do you, Slocum?" The worry in Bennigan's voice told Slocum all he needed to know.

"You saved me. That's what matters. And did the 'coon get your booze?"

"Nope, I—" Bennigan stared at him. "How'd you know that was a whiskey-stealin' racoon?"

"That's about the only thing that'd make you leave me like that," Slocum said, laughing.

"Here, have a snort." Bennigan held out his precious whiskey. Slocum took a small nip and returned it to the miner.

"What are you gonna do? 'Bout me and the Holey?"

"I offered you a mountain of money and you turned it down. That ends the job for me. It's between you and the judge now. You should take the money, though, since he'll find enough loopholes to close around your neck like a noose. He wants the mine, he's not going to stop until he gets it."

"Over my dead body!"

Slocum nodded. He wasn't sure he wouldn't stand beside Bennigan when it came to that. From what the judge said about having to get the mine in weeks, if he missed his deadline he might not want the mine at all. Marshal Delgado was all shot up and didn't have a deputy. Slocum couldn't see Tunstell's law clerk being much good in a gunfight. Alton would never put on a badge to come after Slocum. The rest of the town was just too downright peaceable for the judge to foreclose without a fight he might lose.

For once, Slocum felt that time was on his side. But why did the judge and his partners want the mine at all?

"Where'd he go?" Slocum asked the judge's clerk. Morris peered up at him with his rheumy eyes and nervously licked his lips.

"Don't know, can't say," the man said. "He left real early."

"What about the mayor?"

"Him, too. Him and the judge."

"And Williams?" Slocum saw the clerk shake his head

furiously. This one he did not know and moreover did not care. Slocum left the office and looked around the courthouse. It was as if a holiday had been declared. With both judge and mayor gone for the day—or however long—the majority of the employees had taken the day off. Slocum couldn't blame them. He wanted to quit, too, but this was an opportunity he could not pass up.

He went outside the courthouse and headed directly for the schoolhouse. As he got there, a string of children came out silently. Each one let out a whoop when they stepped away from the building and then tore off like they had been set on fire. Slocum waited until Angela came out. She pushed her hair back and looked as if she had been through a fire. Dark smudges on one cheek added to the impression. Her chestnut hair was in disarray and her clothing was wrinkled and mussed, as if she had been wrestling a grizzly bear.

"What does the loser look like?" Slocum asked.

"John," she said, startled. "I didn't see you. What do you mean?"

"You look like you've gone fifty rounds of bare-knuckle. Since you're still on your feet, you must be the winner."

"I don't feel it," she said, sinking back against the school door. "They are devils. All of them. Someone set off a smoke bomb." She touched the smudge on her cheek. "I had hardly put that out when—oh, never mind. I totally lost control of them all."

"So you sent them home early?"

"They won't go home. They'd have to do chores. It'll be our little secret. They get out early and I don't have to deal with them—and nobody will know."

"You're about the first teacher I ever heard of who couldn't control her class."

"I need a whip."

"Heard that works on some children. Maybe not the boys, but certainly the girls," Slocum said, grinning. Angela found nothing humorous and said so.

"So," she went on, "what brings you by? You look a bit the worse for wear yourself. Was last night that tiring for you?"

"You wore me down," Slocum said.

"Oh, no, not that. I might have worn you out but never down. You're too big for that." She finally smiled.

"Most of city hall's gone. The judge and mayor are off on a trip somewhere. I wondered if you would help me search the city records."

"Search them?" Angela asked, frowning. "Whatever for?"

"Can't rightly say. That's why I need help." Slocum quickly explained the situation with Cal Bennigan and his Holey Mine.

"They want it pretty bad, don't they?" Angela asked.

"Seems like it, but I can't figure out why. Even Bennigan admits he is barely scraping out a living from the gold. I saw the ore he pulled out." He shook his head.

"What do you want me to do?" Angela actually blushed. "Right now, I mean. Later, we can explore other things you might want me to do."

"I want to go over the records and see if there's any hint about what makes that land so valuable that Williams would actually offer me money to kill Bennigan."

"The son of a bitch," Angela said. She ground her teeth together, then said, "I shouldn't say things like that, but he does not seem like a nice man."

"Nice man," mused Slocum. "That's a description that never occurred to me."

"Let's hurry, John. The sooner we finish the search, the sooner we can . . ." She let the sentence trail off, but Slocum understood. And approved.

They got to the courthouse just as Morris locked the door and turned to leave. Slocum grabbed the keys from the man's hand. Before he could protest, Slocum hushed him.

"It'll be all right. The judge won't care."

"My keys," the man said. "He'll skin me alive if I give them over to you."

"He'll do more than that if he finds you left work early. It's not even close to sundown," Slocum pointed out. He opened the door, then tossed the keys back to the clerk. Morris mumbled to himself as he left.

"Going straight to the Desert Oasis, unless I miss my bet," Slocum said.

"No argument. Are all the others there?" Angela looked around the deserted building as if she had never seen it from the inside. He almost asked if it looked different from this side of the mayor's window but did not want to anger her.

"The record books are over there, next to the judge's office," Slocum said. He held the door for her and appreciated the way she smelled as she pushed past. There might have been a lingering gunpowder smell from the smoke bomb, but beneath it all was a perfume that made his heart beat a little faster.

"Let me see," she said, looking over a map spread on a table. "These are the map coordinates." She went to a larger map on the wall and finally located Bennigan's mine after some searching. Her finger stabbed down. "From this we can go to the proper record book."

"Lead on," Slocum said as he looked out into the lobby to be certain the clerk had not returned to spy on them. The building was empty, save for the two of them.

He turned back in time to see her standing with her hands on a book she had taken from a long bookcase.

"Well?"

"Rules of the game, John," she said. "I find this information for you, then you find something for me."

"Wouldn't mind doing that," Slocum said, thinking of all the things Angela might have hidden that they both would like him to search for.

Angela smiled, flipped open the book and spent the next ten minutes comparing numbers from the map to entries in the record book. She frowned and shook her head.

"I don't understand this. Somebody's bought all the land surrounding Bennigan's mine."

"Tunstell, Grierson and Williams?" It was not much of a leap of faith. Slocum was surprised at the answer.

"No, some company called the Mojave East Farming Company."

"Farming? In this country? It's dry as a bone."

"I can find who owns the company."

"Go on," he said, watching as Angela moved through the files, making notes and going to other cabinets filled with stacks of paper. Her trim form moving back and forth, sometimes silhouetted by the light and other times half hidden in shadow, kept Slocum occupied. When she let out a cry of satisfaction, he jumped.

"What is it?"

"You guessed right on the owners of the company. It's really complex. They have hidden their tracks but the judge, banker and mayor own the Mojave East."

"I'd heard the judge say something once about missing it back East where he had orchards," Slocum said.

"Cherry trees," Angela said unexpectedly. "He said something to me about cherry trees and how he wanted to raise them."

"Talk about a fool's errand."

"They are spending a considerable sum to buy up all that land." Angela's finger traced the region on the wall map. "I can't think of any of the men as fools."

"Maybe Williams," Slocum said. The woman's reaction took him aback.

"He's a cold-blooded murderer," she snapped. "He's a coward and—" Angela cut off her tirade, then contritely said, "Sorry. I didn't mean to go on like that." She took a deep breath, settled herself and said, "I found what you wanted. Now you have to find what I want."

"Where do we go?"

"That's the problem. I'm not sure. But I know where to begin."

Slocum took a step forward, intent on showing her where he wanted to begin, but she whirled away and her finger stabbed down on the map again.

"We start here," she said. It took Slocum a few seconds to orient himself on the map.

"Are you certain? That's the route the bank robber used to get out of town after the last robbery."

"I'm sure. I've got a score to settle with him."

Slocum looked at her. Angela was determined. And he had promised, although what she wanted was different from what he had expected.

"You have a horse? No buggies in that country."

"I'll meet you at the stable in fifteen minutes." She paused, gave him a quick kiss and then was gone, leaving behind only the faint odor of gunpowder and perfume.

Slocum took one last look at the area outlined on the map from Angela's clever searching of the records and shook his head. The area owned by Mojave East held most of the gold mining claims—and all of the abandoned mines except Bennigan's. It didn't make sense.

Slocum went to the stables and saddled Conchita for the ride south and around back into the maze of hills where the robber had hidden. It was also unclear why Angela wanted to find the robber. Her venom when Roger Williams was mentioned had to be part of it, but Slocum was too tired to figure it all out. He checked to be sure he had a full cylinder in his Colt Navy, then made certain he had a couple of spare boxes of ammo for the rifle he had slid into the saddle sheath. Going up against the outlaw without enough firepower didn't sit well with him after he had two horses shot out from under him, probably by the same man.

"Don't worry, old girl," Slocum said, patting Conchita on the neck. "You won't go down like that."

"I'm not sure I want to know what you meant, John." Angela stood in the door of the livery, reins trailing from one hand.

"I'm sick of having the damned outlaws shoot my horses," he said. "That's not going to happen this time."

"I hope not," Angela said fervently. Then she grinned. "It would be ever so much more fun if *I* went down . . . on you."

"After we find your robber?"

"You sound doubtful it will happen. It will, John, it will."
Steely determination came into Angela's voice.

"Why do you want to find the robber?"

"He's got something of mine," she said.

"From the bank robbery?" Slocum considered. It had to
be from the second robbery since Angela had not been in
town when the first one had occurred.

"Let's ride," she said.

Slocum tried a few times to engage her in conversation.
He was itching with curiosity over her reasons for finding
the bank robber. When he reached the trail leading into the
hills, though, he stopped trying to pry the information from
her and began concentrating on tracking. It was dark now
and finding the trail was more difficult, even with the moonlight.

"I've found hoofprints but don't know if they belong to
the robber or someone else. The posse came this way when
we found the strongbox."

"I know," Angela said, "but you rode toward town. These
are going into the hills, aren't they?"

Slocum looked up at her and wondered. Angela sat
astride her horse as if she had been born there. She had ridden well. Slocum had expected the hothouse flower Eastern
schoolmarm to have trouble in the saddle. Angela had shown
herself to be a decent horsewoman, riding easily and flowing
with the motion of the horse.

"Where's this going to take us?"

"Into the hills," she said, pointing. "Over there."

"That's off the trail leading to where we found the robber's camp."

"There," she insisted.

Slocum walked along the trail, doing his best to follow increasingly faint hoofprints. The tracks vanished entirely on
him along a rocky patch. More than once he looked in the
direction Angela had pointed. If a man wanted to hide there,
he would have ridden across the patch of rock to hide his trail.

Slocum began to edge toward the hills and ignored the better traveled trail.

He found a pile of fresh horse flop.

"Someone's been here recently," he said. "Not more than a few hours. How'd you know?"

"I'm a schoolteacher. I know everything," she said.

"Tell me right now. You dived in on this trail like a hawk screaming down to pick off a rabbit. No mistakes, straight here."

"Yeah, tell me how you came to find my trail so easy," came a cold voice.

Slocum spun, hand going for his six-shooter, but he froze when he saw he was looking down the barrel of a rifle. The man sighting along the barrel was belly-down on top of a boulder and presented no target at all. He could get off a couple shots before Slocum could clear leather.

Slocum slowly reached for the sky.

14

Slocum waited for the bullet that would end his life. The bank robber who'd shot Jackson Kinney had never slowed down. He was also suspected of killing his partner as he sat locked up in Marshal Delgado's jail as well as shooting Delgado later. With a history like that, the robber had nothing to lose gunning Slocum down.

"You don't have to kill the girl," Slocum said.

"What? What's that you said?" The gunman rose from his spot on the boulder and momentarily silhouetted himself against the night sky. The shadowy outline was too faint for Slocum to take the chance, go for his six-shooter and try to kill the robber. He felt the rifle sights still centered on his chest. Nevertheless, if it saved Angela . . .

"She just came along because she was curious. If she goes back to Dry Water, she won't be able to tell them anything." More bitterly Slocum added, "The only one in town able to track you is all laid up with your bullet in him."

"The marshal? I never shot Delgado."

"He was shot trying to stop you from robbing the bank a second time. What did you get out of that? There couldn't have been any money left in the safe."

"I was already on my way out of town when Delgado was shot."

"John—" Angela put her hand on Slocum's arm. He shrugged it off, hoping she would move behind him so she would be out of the line of fire.

"That's what Bennigan said." Slocum remembered how the miner had said he saw the robber riding out of town when shots at the bank were fired. Slocum had thought there must have been two flurries of gunfire with Delgado being wounded during the robbery. But what caused the second shot if the robber was already out of range? Maybe someone in town had spotted the robber escaping and had opened up on him.

"I went in and had my say with Williams," the robber said. "I was already out and on my horse, halfway out of town when I heard the gunfire."

"Believe him, John. It's true. All of it."

"Did you see the robbery? You should have been teaching."

"There was only a trio of shots," Angela said. "Marshal Delgado was hit three times in the back."

"I hadn't heard that," Slocum said. Angela had no reason to lie about something so easily checked.

"It's so, John. And he didn't have anything to do with killing Marcus, either."

"Marcus?"

"The prisoner in Delgado's jail." The rifleman edged around. Slocum saw movement, blackness within shadow, and knew the robber was coming down. If he had the chance, he could throw down on him and maybe not die instantly.

"No, John. Don't." Angela grabbed his gun hand and held on fiercely. "You don't understand."

"Understand what?"

"Tell him, Hank."

"He's obviously sweet on you, Angel. You can talk to him better than I ever could. And why the hell did you come out here? I told you to steer clear of me."

Slocum looked from the nebulous shape of the gunman to Angela. Her pale face glowed in the moonlight.

"He called you Angel."

"That's his pet name for me. Always has been," she said. "Hank is my brother."

"He's the robber?"

"One of them," Angela said. "Marcus and Leonard were the others."

"Marcus and Leonard Enwright, by any chance?"

"Not Enwright," she said sheepishly. "I sort of switched tickets with the real Miss Enwright. She ended up in Kansas and I came here."

"I don't understand," Slocum said.

"My brothers have been robbing banks for months and not doing a good job of it, I might add," she said angrily. "I was coming after them. I'd only money to buy a ticket to Kansas City. I talked at length with Miss Enwright—"

"She was in her fifties?"

"Oh, yes, quite old," Angela said. "We got to talking because our first names were the same. It was pure chance she was coming to Dry Water. I saw my chance and took it, switching our tickets. The last I'd heard, my brothers were working over in Barstow and I figured I could contact them somehow if I found a spot to hunker down in the area. It was coincidence that they robbed the Dry Water bank before I got there, too late to help them."

"There ain't that many banks out here. And it wasn't our fault, Angel," Hank said contritely. "There was no way we coulda done anything. There wasn't any money."

"Be quiet," she said tartly. "I've never taught school before, but I thought it would be the perfect way to hide in plain sight and find them."

"What did you intend to do when you found them?" Slocum asked.

"Help them plan their robberies better. I think it's a good idea for me to go into a town as a schoolmarm, find what I can from the children, then pass along the information. But it'll be mighty hard doing so now that Marcus and Len are worm food."

Slocum saw tears turning to bright crystal on her cheeks. "What's your real name?"

"Does it matter, John?" She heaved a sigh and said, "Ross."

"Angela Ross," Slocum said, letting the name roll over his tongue. "And you're Hank Ross?"

"Reckon so," the robber said uneasily. "Angel, are you sure it's all right telling him all this?"

"We have to trust someone sometime, Hank. There's no one else in Dry Water."

"So you're part of a gang of bank robbers?" Slocum asked Angela.

"That's right, John," she said. "All of them are my brothers. And that son of a bitch Williams is responsible for killing the two of them!"

"He shot Leonard. That one was fair enough, I reckon, 'cuz it was during the robbery," Hank said, coming closer. Slocum saw that he did not lower his rifle. Hank Ross was alert to any move Slocum might try. "We were trying to rob his damn bank, after all."

"But he killed Marcus. There's no other way our brother could have been gunned down in that cell," Angela said. Her anger mounted. Red spots showed on her cheeks now as emotion took her.

"You didn't get ten thousand in the robbery, did you?" Slocum asked.

"Ten thousand?" Hank Ross snorted in disgust. "I hardly got a hundred. For such a paltry take, I've lost two brothers."

"What happened?"

"Go on," Angela said to her brother. "Tell him. I trust him."

"Trust him because you're screwing him, Angel?"

"He's about the only honest man in Dry Water."

"As if you'd know an honest man if you saw one," Hank said.

"She might be your sister, but that's no way to talk to her."

"So you're defending her honor? That's rich."

Slocum moved like a striking snake. He shifted right just a little, then took two quick steps and went left. His fist aimed straight for Hank Ross's head but this was a feint, too. Slocum kicked at just the right spot and caught the gunman behind the knee. Ross lost his balance, and his rifle muzzle pointed upward, as Slocum swarmed in. Slocum drove his knee into the fallen man's belly as he twisted the rifle away from Hank's hands.

"Now," Slocum started. He felt something cold pressing behind his ear.

"I will shoot, John. You are a good lover, but Hank's my brother. Blood is thicker than water."

"Glad to know what I mean to you," Slocum said, backing off a little. Hank Ross choked and gasped on the ground, struggling to get this breath back. When he did, he sat up, grabbed for his rifle—and found himself staring down the barrel of Angela's derringer.

"He's trying to help, Hank. Settle down now. We can talk this out and not kill each other."

"Like hell," Ross said. He looked pissed but wasn't going to argue. Slocum got the impression that Angela would shoot her own brother if it came to that.

"Thanks," Slocum said.

"There's nothing to thank me for, John Slocum," she said hotly. "I want revenge on Roger Williams and I'm going to get it. I need your help."

"I don't hire out to kill people, even skunks like Williams." Slocum paused a moment, then added, "Even if it would be a godsend for the people of Dry Water."

"Don't turn your back on him," Ross said. "That's the way Leonard got shot."

Slocum said nothing to this. He knew that in the heat of a robbery, front or back got confused and meant nothing. He couldn't hold Williams responsible for shooting Leonard Ross in the back, but if Angela and her brother were right, it was Williams who had shot down Marcus in the jail cell.

This jibed with Slocum's theory that the fleeing robber, the one he and Marshal Delgado had tracked to the fork in the road, could not have doubled back to commit the murder.

"You don't look too upset over the Ross family's business," Angela said.

"How involved have you been up 'til now?"

"I don't put on a mask and go into the bank, if that's what you mean," Angela said. "I can do my part, though. Somebody has to make certain they get away clean. Somebody has to plan the robbery." Angela sounded angry now.

"But you steal strongboxes, don't you?" Slocum asked.

"How did you know?" Her eyebrows arched in surprise.

"I'd already figured out that Grierson stuck up the stage. He was double-crossing the judge by stealing the papers needed to throw Bennigan off his land."

"I found the box where the mayor stashed it just outside town and took it," Angela admitted. "I knew where Hank was camped then. Before he left the camp without bothering to tell me where he had gone." She glared at her brother for such a lack of trust.

"There wasn't anything in the box, was there?"

"As empty as a whore's promise," Hank Ross said.

"As empty as a politician's promise," Angela amended.

"Why'd you rob the bank a second time?" Slocum asked. "That's been eating away at me."

"That's easy. Williams lied about us getting so much money. I thought he must have that much hidden away and was trying to deal off the bottom of the deck."

"Stealing from his partners," Slocum said. "Stealing from that company of theirs."

"The Mojave East Farming Company," Angela said. "Williams had their entire working capital! And he stole it! That's the only explanation for the vault being empty."

"That's why he shot your brother in the jailhouse. He didn't want anyone knowing you hadn't gotten away with that much."

"It wasn't in the bank when I went back, either. I got more

than the first time, but not much. Maybe four hundred dollars, but nothing close to ten thousand."

"That amount rolled right off Williams's tongue right after the robbery. I thought it was kind of glib. He knew exactly how much had been taken without going over his books to figure it out."

"But John, what are we going to do?" asked Angela. "He murdered our two brothers. He stole the money from his own partners. Williams can't get away with it."

"If I told Judge Tunstell, I'm not sure there would be much he could do. He might be sharp when it comes to business dealings, but he's honest to a fault when it comes to the law. Without proof, he wouldn't do a thing."

"So he uses the law to steal. Is that different from using a gun to hold up a bank?" demanded Angela.

"It's less honest," her brother said. "There's no risk to him, but he steals just the same."

"Tunstell can't or won't do anything unless we can prove the charges against Williams. Chances are mighty good that Williams shot the marshal in the back, too."

"The marshal might have figured out what Williams had done," Ross said.

"Delgado's in no condition to get proof for the judge now," said Slocum.

"I think the mayor's in cahoots with Williams. He robbed the stage himself to get those papers," Angela said. "He must be helping Williams. He might be the one who shot down Marcus. It could be either Williams or Grierson. They have motive enough."

"Might be," Slocum said slowly, "and maybe he's trying to grab Bennigan's property for himself. He must have figured out that you didn't get all their company's money in the first robbery. Grierson isn't so dumb that he would believe Williams, so he knows he's being robbed in plain sight. This could be his way of getting back at the banker in a way Williams can't fight." He looked at Angela and Hank. "Do either of you know why that worthless mine is so important to them?"

Angela and Hank looked at each other, then shook their heads. Slocum settled down and thought about all that they had said. He believed them. Their anger at the deaths of their two brothers was not faked.

"What do we do, John?" Angela came to him and laid her hand on his shoulder. She kept the derringer in her other hand where she could use it if the need arose.

"Proof is needed if we are going to turn them over to the law," Slocum said.

"If Tunstell's mixed up in this, he's not going to listen," said Hank.

"You're right," Slocum allowed, "if he knows half of what's going on. He might suspect. Or he might be too intent on his own schemes to notice everything around him." Slocum had to admit he liked Tunstell, and this colored his opinion of the man. Or Tunstell might be the brains behind it all. He had probably set up the legal corporation and had figured out how to bamboozle Bennigan out of his land, but murder? Robbery from his partners? Slocum wasn't sure those fit with how Tunstell operated.

"What would serve as proof?"

"You didn't see the mayor dump the box, did you?"

"No, John, I didn't. But I could lie and say that I did."

"Won't matter. The strongbox was found in the camp of a suspected bank robber. I never bothered to tell Tunstell my suspicions about who robbed the stagecoach." Slocum turned to Hank and asked, "What color are your eyes?"

"What kind of crazy question is that, Slocum?"

"Blue," said Angela. "Stop dragging your feet, Hank. John is trying to help."

"Why?"

"I know you didn't rob the stage. The robber had brown eyes. Like Grierson. But this is thin evidence. The judge could argue that you didn't do the robbing but a partner did."

"My eyes are green," Angela said.

"Don't even hint that you're in cahoots with the robbers. Given half a chance, Williams and Grierson will see your pretty neck stuck into a noose," Slocum said. "We need evidence. The center of all this is Bennigan's claim. If we find what the Mojave East Farming Company wants with it, we have a motive. It all unravels."

"It's likely to catch up your friend the judge," Hank said. "He's not lily-white in this. He's as dirty as Grierson and Williams."

"Might be. Let's see what we can find out," Slocum said, "by nosing around and getting documents. I would surely like to see what the papers Tunstell was sending to Sacramento were."

"You told me copies were on the way but wouldn't be here for weeks."

"For weeks . . ." Slocum mused, "and Tunstell is in a powerful hurry to get Bennigan off his claim fast."

"Why are you rambling on and on about this played-out gold mine?" cried Hank. "Williams killed two of my brothers. I want revenge on him."

"You could have gunned him down the instant you walked into the bank if you didn't want more from him," Slocum said.

"That's damned straight, Slocum," Hank Ross said. "I want him to suffer. I want him to know he's lost his precious money. *Then* I want him dead."

Slocum looked at the night sky and judged the path of the moon and where the stars had moved.

"It'll be dawn in an hour. If we ride like the wind, we can get back to town before anyone shows up at the courthouse. More nosing around might help."

"I don't know if we can get there in time, John," Angela said. "That snotty clerk of Tunstell's always shows up early. He's a real ass kisser."

Slocum motioned for them to mount. He and Angela had to wait for Ross to get to his horse and join them. Then they galloped for town. Angela's estimate of how long it would take them to arrive proved closer than Slocum's. Not only was the sun already up and bringing more summer heat to Dry Water, but from the horses tethered behind the courthouse, both Tunstell and Grierson had returned.·

"So much for that. We can wait until tonight," Angela said.

"The window's open. I see two men in there."

"The mayor's office," Angela said. She cast a quick look at Slocum, imploring him not to mention how she had been eavesdropping at that very spot.

"Let's see what we can find out," Hank Ross said. He looked at them, perplexed. "What? You don't want to take the risk of being seen? It doesn't matter to me. Nobody in town knows me."

"Except by your shirt," Slocum said. "That pattern's burned into everyone's head as belonging to the bank robber."

"Screw it," Hank said. "No guts, no glory."

"We can keep people from noticing him, John," Angela said. "Let Hank try." She put her hand on his arm and held him back before he could stop her impetuous brother.

"What's there to lose?" Slocum wondered aloud. He motioned for Angela to join him at the front of the courthouse while her brother sneaked to the side to get under the mayor's open window. What there was to learn would never be useful in convincing Tunstell, but Hank might implicate the judge and remove any hint of loyalty Slocum felt for him.

"Should we create a scene, John?" Angela smiled brightly. "I know just the way to distract people."

"You're already distracting me," Slocum said. She had unbuttoned her blouse so that the tops of her ample bosom almost spilled out. The snowy expanse of succulent flesh made Slocum wonder what she was enticing him to do.

"I know how to draw the whole town's attention," Angela said. "I think we can get *most* of them watching and that'll be good enough."

They dismounted and went up to the door leading into the

courthouse where Angela threw her arms around his neck and planted a big wet kiss on his lips.

"Go on," she whispered. "Act like you enjoyed it." She kissed him again.

Slocum wasn't able to see out into the street but he felt all eyes turning toward them. Even if Hank Ross painted himself purple and jumped up and down waving his arms, nobody would notice him under the mayor's window. What was going on so blatantly in front of God and everyone on the courthouse steps would be talked about for months.

The schoolmarm and the drifter! Kissing! Scandalous!

"Hmmm, nice," Angela said, stepping away from him and looking up into his eyes. "Gives me ideas for more. A lot more."

"Do you think we ought to . . . attract some more attention?"

Angela laughed. "I don't know how long Hank needs but—"

The words were hardly out of her mouth when her brother screamed, "You damned murderer! You killed Marcus!"

The gunshot sent a chill up Slocum's back. Kissing in public would entertain the people of Dry Water. The sound of gunfire would make them all drag out their own six-shooters.

15

"Wait!" Slocum grabbed Angela's arm and kept her from running around the side of the courthouse. "You can't do anything for him there."

"But John, I have to do something."

Slocum looked across the street and saw curious men emerging from their businesses. The saloon had only a few customers this early in the morning, but the general store had a half dozen and all came out with their hands resting on six-guns or gripping rifles.

Another shot broke glass.

"You killed him, you filthy son of a bitch!"

"John, please!" Angela tried to pull free, but he swung her around and shoved her toward the open courthouse doors.

"Inside. We have to head him off. Whoever he's shooting at's not going to stay in the office." He herded her ahead of him into the lobby of the courthouse. Two men had already stumbled from the mayor's office. Slocum wasn't surprised to see Grierson and Roger Williams.

"Slocum, thank God!" cried the mayor. "Somebody's shooting at me through the window. Damn near plugged me, too."

137

"It's me they were shooting at," insisted the banker. "It's the bank robber come back to finish the job. They're outside, Slocum. Get them. He's there!"

"How many?" Slocum said, sowing what discord he could. "Three or four?"

"One, no two, I don't know," Williams said. He pressed his back against the wall and looked as if he had seen a ghost. His hands shook, and he was a pasty white. For a moment it looked like the banker had been on the receiving end of Hank's bullets.

"You're a damn fool, Roger," the mayor said. "Slocum, you're the closest we have to a lawman right now, with the marshal all laid up. Get in there and do something."

"Where's the judge?" Slocum asked. "I was coming to see him."

"I don't know where Tunstell is, and I don't care. He's not the one being shot at," Grierson said angrily.

"You go get to safety," Slocum said to Angela. He pushed her toward the front door and inclined his head in the direction of the window where Hank had opened fire. "Get to safety right now."

Angela nodded quickly, understanding what Slocum was up to. She disappeared. Slocum waited until she headed in the direction of her brother. He hoped the outlaw wouldn't cut down his own sister in his rage.

"I heard yelling. What'd the gunman say?" Slocum asked of the two men, playing for time.

"What's the difference? Get him, Slocum." Grierson pointed to his office. When the man started to go back inside, Slocum grabbed his arm and pulled him away.

"I'll take care of this, Mayor."

Slocum interposed himself between the mayor and the open doorway. He sucked in a deep breath, then inched forward cautiously. He hoped Angela had calmed her brother and convinced him to hightail it. Just inside the door, Slocum leveled his gun at the window and fired. Another pane of glass shattered. He ran to the window and looked out in time to see Angela tugging at Hank Ross's sleeve, getting him to run toward the schoolhouse. If she was smart, and Slocum thought she was, she would hide him there while the hunt went elsewhere.

Slocum fired a couple times in the direction of the crowd approaching from up the street. He got several rounds fired back at him. Only one came close, but it burned hot on his ear from passage. Dropping down, he fired a couple more times and got the crowd all agitated. Only then did he back off and return to the lobby where Grierson and Williams waited nervously.

"Did you get him, Slocum?" asked Williams. "He was gunning for me. I know he was."

"Could be," Slocum said. "There's a bunch of men coming from all over town. I need to make sure none of them gets hurt."

He took three quick strides and got to the open courthouse doors. Waving his bandanna to get the crowd's attention, Slocum yelled, "It's me, Slocum. I've got the mayor and banker here. Don't shoot."

"You come on out and let us see the color of your eyes," Alton called. Slocum kept waving his bandanna as he stepped out.

He swallowed hard when he heard more than a couple hammers going back. Then Alton shouted, "It's not the varmint what tried to rob the bank. It's only Slocum."

"You chased him off," Slocum said loudly enough for even the men at the rear of the crowd to hear. "Get your horses. I'll help you track him down. You still a deputy, Alton?"

Slocum saw the barkeep pause. A dozen conflicting emotions crossed his face. Then he found his backbone.

"I am," he said.

"Then let's get mounted and go after them. You see how many of them there were?"

"I thought there was just the one. I recognized his shirt," Alton said. "It was all checkered blue and white, jist like the bank robber's. I figure it's got to be the same man."

"There was only one outlaw," Grierson said.

"But there could have been more," Williams said. "There was so much shooting going on, I don't see how just one man could be responsible. They were all trying to kill me."

Slocum let the banker and mayor argue a few seconds. He remembered an old toast a friend of his from the war used to give. "Confusion to our enemies." Slocum's mouth was as dry as the Mojave and he wished he could take a good long pull from a bottle of whiskey, but there wasn't any way he could convince the crowd of that. They were a posse on the verge of being a lynch mob. He had to keep them under control until Angela found a way to get her brother out of town.

"Slocum," Grierson said, grabbing his arm, "there was only the one skunk shooting at me and Roger. There's no need to find more 'n the one."

"I'll be careful who we bring back," Slocum said. "Tell the judge what's happened." He paused a moment and asked, "Where is he, anyway?"

Grierson and Williams exchanged looks that told him they knew and weren't likely to reveal it.

"Can't rightly say. Get into the saddle."

"I'll offer a thousand-dollar reward!" Williams shouted out.

"That's mighty generous for a man whose bank lost every last cent to the robbers," Slocum said.

"It . . . it'll be out of the money they stole. It's a reward for the robbers and recovering the money." Williams knew how lame this sounded. "You heard the mayor. Ride, Slocum, ride."

Slocum turned and vaulted into the saddle. Conchita sagged a little under his weight, widened her stance some and then set off at a steady pace Slocum knew could be maintained all day long. Behind him came the townspeople in twos and threes. By the time he reached the edge of town, Alton had galloped up to ride beside him.

"Why're we goin' this way, Slocum? The varmint went toward the school."

"I heard hooves," Slocum lied. "He must have had a horse hidden there. Going this way, we might cut him off."

"Cut him off from what?" Alton looked genuinely perplexed. "You know where he's headin'?"

"Back to the trail we followed into town from his camp up in the hills. He wants to get back up there so he can hide out," Slocum said.

"Why'd he go back to a camp he knows we've already found?"

"There," Slocum said, pointing at the ground. "I was right. Tracks."

Alton leaned over and looked at the bare ground and shook his head. "I don't see nuthin'."

"You're a bartender, not a tracker," Slocum said. He stood in his stirrups and waved his arm forward like a cavalry captain ordering an all-out attack.

The men were so het up they didn't stop to question Slocum. Even Alton got caught up in the rush to find the outlaw who had shot into the courthouse. For the rest of the day Slocum followed game trails and rode them in circles until they were rung out and so tired they could hardly stay in the saddle.

"I'm sorry, boys," Slocum called. "I lost the trail. I had it, but the rocky terrain, the sandy patches, it got too confusing to follow."

"Back to the Desert Oasis to regroup," Alton said. "Drinks are on . . . Slocum."

A weak cheer went up. Slocum glared at Alton but secretly appreciated the offer made in his behalf. He knew exactly where every member of this ragtag posse would go. If he dawdled, they would wait for him—in the saloon. He had done his best to give Hank Ross a head start. If the man was smart, he would be twenty miles away by now.

Slocum turned a little glum when he realized that Angela probably had gone with Ross. Slocum rode slowly back into town, trailing the rest of the posse.

Slocum figured that most of the questions were answered,

but some were still a little fuzzy in his head. Either Grierson or Williams had killed Ross's brother in jail. From the way things had gone down in Dry Water after the robbery, Roger Williams might not have been out of sight of the crowd long enough. That meant Grierson had pulled the trigger on Marcus Ross. Slocum was positive the mayor had robbed the stagecoach and taken Tunstell's eviction papers.

That was the biggest question in Slocum's mind. Why did the trio of politicians that ran Dry Water want a hard-rock miner's claim when there was no gold there? The three were busy double-crossing each other. With a little hint, Slocum wondered if he could get the judge to spill the beans and find out what the Mojave East Farming Company's real purpose had been before lead flew and people died.

He got into town and dismounted in front of Alton's saloon. The Desert Oasis lived up to its name. Men were crowding inside and the click of beer mugs and the clink of shot glasses hitting the bar told him he would have a powerful big bill to pick up. If it meant Hank Ross—and his sister—got away scot-free, it was worth it.

Slocum went in to a rousing cheer. They picked him up and carried him to the bar, as if he were a conquering hero.

"Hey, stop, put me down," he barked. They were hardly listening. Somehow Slocum got his feet under him. "You men did good today, upholding the spirit of the law in Dry Water." Slocum wasn't much for speeches but he had to say something or they would never let him leave. He did not bother pointing out that they had not caught their quarry. If they had, Slocum would have found himself in an uncomfortable position. It would not have taken much to get them to let him pin on a deputy's badge again. With Delgado laid up, he would be in charge of the jailhouse and its prisoners. Ross could escape in the dead of night.

Slocum didn't cotton much to that solution and was glad it had not come to that. Wearing a badge irked him since he had as little truck with lawmen as possible. The ones that didn't want to clap him in jail were crooked. Slocum figured that Marshal Delgado was one of the honest ones and would have put Slocum behind bars if he had seen any of the wanted posters bearing his likeness.

Slocum downed a couple shots of whiskey and felt the warmth spreading throughout his belly. He turned when he heard his name called.

Grierson stood in the door of the saloon, beckoning to him. He wanted nothing to do with the mayor but saw no way to avoid it.

"What can I do for you, Mayor?"

"We followed him," Grierson said angrily.

"Who?" Slocum went cold inside. He had never thought Grierson and Williams would have tried to capture Hank Ross on their own, but it sounded this way.

"You know who. The bank robber. The one who shouted at us and tried to kill us."

"We tracked him but lost the varmint outside town," Slocum said. Grierson wanted none of his excuses.

"You were chasing your own damned tail. I thought you were better than that. Roger and I grabbed our guns and went after him. He lit out toward the schoolhouse. He had a horse tethered behind it. We waited for him." The way Grierson fingered the six-shooter thrust into his belt, Slocum knew what the mayor really meant. Williams and Grierson had wanted to ambush Ross.

"What happened?"

"We must have tipped our hand. He never came for his horse, so that means he's still in Dry Water somewhere. I want you to mount a door-to-door hunt for him."

"That'll rile up the whole town," Slocum said.

"So rile them. I don't want that back-shooting son of a bitch out there free to murder me or Williams. He robbed the bank twice, killed a prisoner, tried to shoot us. I want him, Slocum."

Slocum said nothing. His mind refused to come up with a decent excuse.

"Don't forget, he gunned down your pal Jackson Kinney."

"He wasn't a friend. I just felt sorry for him."

Grierson smiled crookedly, knowing he had hit Slocum where he lived. If Slocum refused to lead the search, it would be tacit admission of being in cahoots with the robbers. Grierson might know that Slocum had recognized him during the stage robbery. This was a clever way of mouse-trapping him.

"I'll get some of the men out hunting," Slocum said. "But they're on their way to getting likkered up something fierce." He pointed to the men at the bar. One of them had already passed out from drinking too much pop skull.

"You do that. I'll tag along to help however I can."

Slocum bellowed to Alton to let somebody else tend bar and to come with him. The barkeep took a few minutes to round up the customers most likely to rob him blind if he left his saloon. In the street, they stood in a wobbly group, supporting each other. Slocum worried that they were so drunk they might shoot anything that moved—including themselves.

"Mayor Grierson says we missed the skunk who tried to shoot him and Williams."

"I tole ya, Slocum," slurred one of the posse. "We missed 'im out south o' town."

"We went north, you idiot," growled Alton. "We had the trail. We just lost it. Right, Slocum?"

"Grierson thinks we can find him hiding here in town." He turned to the mayor. "Where do you think we ought to start?" Before Grierson could answer, Slocum gave the answer. "Over to the bank, men. If the yahoo is the same as what tried to rob the bank before, he might try again."

"Wait, no, he—" Grierson's sputtering orders were ignored as Slocum led the tipsy parade to the bank. He saw Williams inside at his desk, working furiously on a ledger book. The banker jumped as if he had been stuck with a pin when Slocum barged in, followed by Alton and the others.

"What's the meaning of this, Slocum?"

"The mayor ordered us to find the man who took a shot at you."

"He did more than that. He tried to kill me."

"You might just be right. Look around," Slocum told Alton and the others. "Don't leave any place where he might be hiding untouched."

"He's not here. Why are you—stop! You can't go in there!"

Slocum grabbed Williams by the shoulder and shoved him back into his chair.

"It's only the vault. There can't be much inside after two big robberies, right?"

"You can't go there! Get out. All of you, clear out!"

"We just want to be sure you're safe. That owlhoot might be hiding with a six-gun trained on you, forcing you to say things you wouldn't otherwise," Slocum said. "The mayor's worried sick that you might get yourself shot."

Slocum cocked his six-shooter behind the man's head, and Williams jumped a foot. He spun the chair around and smiled at the banker. The smile was more feral than friendly. The expression on the banker's face was worth the effort.

"Judge Tunstell doesn't want anything to happen to you, either," Slocum added.

Slocum wanted to sow as much discord among the partners as he could. Keeping them stirred up and distrustful of each other was the only way he could see for Ross to get out of town—and for a lot of the questions Slocum had to find answers.

"Ain't nobody here but the banker fella," a posse member said.

"Let's keep looking," Slocum said. "We should come back here in a spell to be sure you're all right, Mr. Williams. To keep you and the bank safe."

"There's no need. I—" Williams covered the ledger when Slocum took a long hard look at it. All Slocum saw was the brief glimpse of MOJAVE EAST FARMING COMPANY at the head of the page.

"Don't you fret," Slocum said, leaving the banker to do just that.

Outside, Slocum saw Grierson moving quickly from one

store to the next on the far side of the street. It took some doing but Slocum got his drunken posse to follow Grierson and slowed down his search to a crawl. By the time they had finished with all the businesses and offices along the main street, it was twilight. One by one the posse drifted away to return to the Desert Oasis.

"Got to get back to the saloon, Slocum," Alton said. "If I don't watch the till, them bandits will be drinkin' on the house all night long."

"What about it, Mayor?" Slocum was glad it was dark so Grierson could not see the broad grin on his face. "Keep looking or give up for the night?"

"Go to hell," Grierson said, storming off.

Alton looked puzzled. "What's that all about? We done what we could, me and you and the rest."

"There's no pleasing some people," Slocum said, slapping Alton on the shoulder. "Let's go have a drink."

Slocum sipped at whiskey until after midnight. Most of the town had either passed out or gone home to sleep. It was time for him to find Hank Ross and get him the hell out of Dry Water.

16

The cold desert air sucked the moisture from Slocum as he walked down the middle of Dry Water's main street. He walked slowly, carefully, making it appear that he was drunker than he was. He felt eyes on him but could not locate the source. It had to be Grierson. The mayor had been furious at him for not finding Hank Ross and must have—rightly—figured that Slocum knew the robber's whereabouts.

Slocum let out a huge belch and wandered toward the shadows near the livery stable. Swallowed by the darkness, Slocum swung around and intently watched the buildings across the street. He was only mildly surprised when he saw movement on the roof of the pharmacist's store. Grierson had taken the high ground to watch.

"Smarter than I thought," Slocum said, realizing he dared not underestimate the mayor. The man had robbed the stage and probably had shot Marcus Ross in jail. He was a double-dealer and was crossing Judge Tunstell. Any of those doings made Slocum wary. But the notion that Grierson would kill to protect whatever scheme he was brewing sobered Slocum completely.

Moving cautiously, Slocum went to the rear of the stable.

He ducked in through a window and spent a few minutes laying out his blanket over a pile of straw. He dropped his hat at the top of the bundle. If anyone checked, the deception would be instantly apparent. Slocum hoped Grierson only peered in through the dirty window at the far end of the stall. He moved quietly, patted Conchita, then left through the door he had used to enter the stables.

The night was chilly and silent. Distant singing from a lone crooner in the Desert Oasis was about the only unnatural sound to be heard. Slocum had waited long enough for the moon to just be creeping up over the hills to the east but not so long that he would cast a shadow when he moved. He ran for the courthouse and crouched near the front steps where he had shoved Angela away to rescue her brother.

Using his sense of touch more than sight, he found in the soft dirt the outline of her dainty shoe leading to the side of the building. Staying close to the wall, he inched around until he was directly under Grierson's office window. Bright shards of glass lay everywhere.

He rose slowly and chanced a peek inside the office. Glass was strewn all over Grierson's desk, showing where Ross's bullet had left its tracks. Other than silent echoes of the gunfire, the office was empty. Slocum ducked back down and carefully studied the main street for any sign of Grierson or Williams. He knew they were out prowling around.

At least Grierson was. He wanted Ross so bad he could taste the bitter revenge on his tongue.

Other than a man stumbling down the street, going in the opposite direction, Slocum saw no one stirring in Dry Water. He cast a quick glance in the direction of the schoolhouse. The empty stretch would be hard to cross without being seen if someone still lurked on the rooftops in town. Slocum began walking slowly. He sped up, slowed and occasionally stopped. Anything to keep from rhythmic movement that might draw attention. His broken field walk finally took him to the front steps of the school. He sat on the steps and waited almost ten minutes to catch any sight of someone spying on him.

Slocum had found that a minute or two lying in wait was never long enough. Most men could do that. Five minutes of spying made them edgy. Ten seemed as if someone had set fire to their pants. He doubted Grierson had the patience to wait that long to see what Slocum was up to. The mayor would have to edge closer or otherwise show his hand.

Nothing.

Slocum went to the door into the school and carefully opened it. He heard a hinge begin to squeak. Moving with even greater care, he pushed past the noise until he had opened it enough to slip inside.

The classroom was silent. The settling of the building and soft whistle of wind through a crack somewhere up high were the only sounds Slocum heard. Until a rustling followed by a held breath being forcefully released alerted him to someone else in the shadowy room.

His six-shooter slid easily into his hand. Slocum strained to figure out where the noise came from. Another rustle. He moved like a striking snake. Three quick steps, a turn and he had his six-gun leveled at the person hiding behind a bookcase.

"Angela!"

"Oh, John, it's you. I heard the door hinge squeaking. I worried that it was Grierson again."

"He followed you and Hank here?"

"Of course he did. You got most of the town off on a wild-goose chase, but he was too clever. He followed us straight here. I was already letting the children in for class, so he didn't dare make much of a scene. But he had a gun and he would have used it, no matter he might have hit the children and—"

"Hush," Slocum said, taking her into his arms. She fit perfectly into the circle of his embrace. "It'll be all right. Did Hank get away safely?"

"N-no. I had to hide him. And Williams found his horse and took it. Hank doesn't have any way of getting out of town."

"Hush," Slocum repeated. "Where is he now?"

The woman quaked in his arms as she sobbed out her story of woe. "I hid him. Under the floor."

"He's below us right now?" Slocum stepped back from the woman and looked down at the floorboards. He half expected to see Ross's head poke up to watch them.

"Not here. Over by my desk. He hid in the kneehole just as Grierson came in. Hank pried up a board and got underneath. By then he had to stay since the children were here for class and I couldn't dismiss them. I—"

"I've got to get him out of town. Grierson is still hunting. The son of a bitch is as tenacious as any man I've ever seen."

"He shot at Hank. When Hank missed, he shot back."

"I know." Slocum rapidly went to the desk and shoved it back. He saw the two boards Ross had pried up. Blood stained both and a fingernail was embedded in one, showing how furiously he had worked to pry up the boards to get to safety.

"Come on out, Ross," Slocum said, rapping on the board. "It's me, Slocum. Grierson is still hunting for you so I've got to get you out of town pronto."

The board moved up an inch. Slocum saw an eye reflect some light as Ross peered out to be sure. Then the board lifted and bent until nails pulled free farther down. With a sinuous twist, Hank Ross flopped out onto the classroom floor. He was filthy from the dirt and covered with cobwebs.

"Damn near couldn't stand another second down there. Rather be in my own grave."

"No, Hank, don't say that."

"Angel, you don't know how awful it is trapped under the floor with those whippersnappers moving overhead all day. You wouldn't believe what leaks down, either."

"I might," Angela said, chuckling for the first time.

"Enough of that. Reminisce later," Slocum said. He stood next to the window, watching the street in front of the courthouse for any sign of movement. Dry Water was as silent as a cemetery.

If Grierson found them, the town might have to bury its

victims where they fell. Slocum wanted to make sure his name wasn't going to be on any of those tombstones.

"He might try to take you himself or get help from Alton and the others. It's late and most of them in the saloon are drunk or passed out. That means Grierson and Williams might be all we have to worry over."

"Hank, be careful." Angela hugged her brother, then sneezed. She pushed him to arm's length and looked him over. "You are filthy."

"I told you," Ross said.

"Let's go. We're going to steal a couple of the mayor's horses."

"Angela said the banker took mine. I want that mare back." Ross squared his shoulders and looked ready for a fight. Slocum knew the man wanted to strike back at his tormentors.

"Why'd you take a shot at Grierson in the first place?"

"He confessed. As God is my witness, he told Williams he had pulled the trigger and killed Marcus!"

"You'll want to get away so you can do something about it. Grierson is the mayor of this town and carries some clout. All he has to do is say the word and the townsfolk would string you up," Slocum said.

"Yes, he's right, Hank. Go now and then we can figure out how to get even with Grierson later."

"There's only one way of getting even with him." Ross put his hand on the oak grips of his six-shooter. Slocum had to agree, but he had other fish to fry. For the first time it came to him that he might be helping in the escape of the man who killed Jackson Kinney during the first robbery. Old Jack had been a harmless coot and deserved more than a stray bullet.

"Come on," Slocum said, feeling a little less inclined to help Ross. He'd still get him out of town, but then the outlaw was on his own.

"Good-bye, Hank," Angela said. She gave her brother a quick kiss on the cheek. The one she gave Slocum was anything but quick, and it was full on the lips.

Slocum got uncomfortable knowing her brother watched. He didn't know if she wanted to assert some independence, show Hank she was her own woman, or if it was merely a way of angling for control over him. Even as Slocum thought that, he damned himself for being so suspicious. Too much scheming had gone on in town for him to avoid some of it rubbing off on him.

He broke free and went to the door. He peered out into the night. The moon had risen enough to cast muted shadows and cause bright silver reflections off shiny objects. If Grierson was prowling about, he might easily see them.

"Pretend that you're drunk," Slocum said. "Head for the corral behind the courthouse. That's where they most likely put your horse."

"If we run, it'll get us there quicker," Ross said.

"I want to keep Grierson guessing. He sees a pair of drunks, he's not as likely to investigate as if he sees two cowboys on foot running like the devil's after their asses."

Ross nodded once. He sucked in a deep breath and then stepped outside. Slocum followed, closing the door. Angela opened it to follow.

"Stay here," Slocum said. "I'll be back soon."

"Hurry, John. I . . . I'll be waiting for you." The sight of her bathed in the light of the full moon made Slocum think once more of angels.

He put his arm around Ross's shoulder and started off at an unsteady gait. The two of them fell into a pattern of moving apart and coming back together that Slocum thought was convincing. The entire way to the corral he worried that Grierson might spot them and simply shoot them down. He saw nothing, and Grierson never put in an appearance.

"There she is," Ross said, abandoning the pretense of drunkenness. He vaulted over the corral fence and landed next to his mare.

Slocum found the man's gear and pushed it along the top rail for him to saddle up. Knowing Ross would be ready to ride in a few minutes, Slocum found himself a decent mount and saddled it. Then he cut out a third horse from those in the corral. He threw a bridle on it and led it from the corral.

"Why take another horse, Slocum?"

"You'll see." Slocum rode at a trot away from the courthouse and found a back trail. Ross followed at a distance, as if wary of a trap. Slocum reached a fork in the trail. One branch went back toward the main road for Pemberton. He swatted the rump of the spare horse and got it running away.

"Diversion?"

"Let them follow three trails," Slocum said.

"Three? You're not coming with me?"

"I've got business back in Dry Water," Slocum said.

"Slocum," began Hank Ross. The outlaw got up his courage. "You do right by Angela. If anything happens to me, you do right by her."

"You're going to get away. Head into the hills and make a camp. Stay out of sight for a few days. By then, the pot will either have boiled over or the fire'll have gone cold."

"Good luck," Ross said, thrusting out his hand.

Slocum hesitated, then shook. "Good luck to you, too."

The outlaw took off to find a hideout in the hills bordering the Mojave. Slocum waited for him to get out of sight, then rode around in circles for a spell, kicking up dust and camouflaging the trail. Grabbing a hunk of sage, he used it to erase bits of trail all around. This wouldn't stop any decent tracker but would slow down the pursuit.

Slocum eventually headed across country, ignoring trails in favor of open desert. The hard sand barely took his horse's hoofprints. But anyone hunting would find three different directions to follow. Knowing Alton and the rest of the posse as well as he did, he doubted they would be willing to split into thirds and go after each supposed rider.

Slocum circled around, came into Dry Water from the west and then returned the horse to the corral. There was no reason for him to steal a horse. If Tunstell wanted to argue the case in court, should it ever happen, it could be argued the one missing horse belonging to Grierson had simply gotten out when Ross retrieved his own horse. But such a minor crime would never be put in front of the judge. Not when bigger ones were being hatched—and by the judge himself.

Slocum heaved the saddle over the top rail of the corral fence and quickly made his way back to the schoolhouse. Again he waited some time before going in, just to be certain Grierson wasn't laying a trap for him. When the door hinge squeaked this time, there was an immediate response from inside.

"You took your sweet time getting back, John."

"Had to cover tracks and—" He became speechless when he saw Angela. She stood gloriously naked in the moonlight. Her entire body was a pure silver, with shadows in the most intimate of spots. Her nipples were erect and cast tiny shadows on the bottoms of her breasts. Her belly was flat and delightful and her legs moved slowly, moving back and forth like the blades of some ivory scissors.

"Come here."

"What if it hadn't been me?" Slocum asked as he shed his gun belt and tossed aside his shirt. He was peeling down his trousers as she came to him.

"I would have been forced to make up a good story. But you came back before that happened."

"I know why," he said, reaching out and cupping her breasts. They were warm and alive, not like the cold, silvery stone they appeared to be in the moonlight.

He caught the nipples and twisted them back and forth. She moaned softly and thrust her chest forward, crushing down hard into the palms of his hands. Her eyes closed and her head tipped back. When her lips parted in obvious invitation, Slocum kissed her. The kiss was hard and passionate, then grew in intensity until he thought he would burst.

She threw her arms around his neck to hold him in place. Their lips worked feverishly and then her tongue came snaking out to lightly caress his. He returned the invitation with a bolder intrusion into her mouth. Their tongues frolicked back and forth, dancing and rolling over one another until they both were gasping for breath.

"Go on, John. Finish. Get naked for me."

He kicked off his boots, and she helped skin him out of his jeans. He sighed with relief when his quivering erection was freed from its cloth prison. She saw his hardness immediately and pounced on it like a dog on a bone. Her mouth closed over the purpled tip and she began kissing and licking until Slocum thought he would go crazy with need. His balls tightened and deep inside he felt the rising tide of his come.

He ran his fingers through her lustrous hair, now glinting with shiny highlights in the moon, and pushed her face away from his crotch. She looked up. Her eyes danced with lust.

"Your mouth feels too good on me to keep up for much longer."

"Then you should do something to take your mind off it," she said. Rising gracefully, she struck a pose. "Whatever might that be?" Angela turned and presented her sleek ass cheeks to him. He reached out and stroked over them, only to have her step out of reach. "You must think of other things, John. What would you like to think about? Other than this?"

She ran her hands across her breasts, down over her stomach and then stroked through the tangled bush between her thighs. She sighed in pleasure as she began stroking in and out of herself with a long middle finger.

"This is soooo nice," she said. "But my finger feels . . . tiny. I would be so much more filled with your cock in me."

She backed away another couple steps and perched on the edge of her desk. Angela leaned back and hiked her feet to the edge as she rocked backward. Her knees parted, giving him a delicious view of paradise.

"You might lick me there," she said. "Or something else. You could put something other than your tongue there. Oh! Oh, yes!"

He moved into the V of her legs, running his work-hardened hands down the soft insides until he reached the spot she so wantonly put on display for him and him alone. Slocum slid a little closer and braced himself in either side of her hips. She grabbed between her own legs and caught his fleshy stalk. Her fumbling fingers guided him forward until he touched the damp nether lips protecting her inner glories.

"Do it, John darling. Do it."

She let out a gasp of pure delight when he slid in easily, moving smoothly forward, burying himself deep within her. The tightness increased as she gasped and moaned, her passions building. Her inner oils made her slick enough for him to slip in and out a few inches with only a small effort. The slight stroking movement caused her to flop back onto the desk. Her head rolled from side to side, sending her lustrous hair flying in what looked like a halo around her head.

He looked down at her and watched her begin to fondle her own breasts. Then she tensed her strong inner muscles, and Slocum knew she was more devil than angel in this instant. The pressure all around him caused him to withdraw, but only for a moment to catch his breath.

His hips levered forward, and he buried himself in her once more. He began moving faster, with more power, giving her what she wanted. The friction along his shaft mounted and even burned as he thrust faster. Slocum heaved himself forward and felt their crotches press together. He withdrew more slowly to torment her, but it also gave him an electric thrill that he could not deny.

"John, I—" Angela arched her back and crammed herself down harder around him. He began thrusting with all the power and speed locked within his loins. The world spun around him and then all sensation began to pool in his loins. He bent forward, ran his hands under her shoulders and used this to lever himself for even harder thrusts. His world vanished in a wild surge of pleasure, then he began to turn limp within her clinging interior.

"Oh, John, I didn't want it to ever stop."

"Not made of steel," he said.

"I'm glad. What you have is all hard and warm. No, not warm. Hot."

He tried to rise, but she grabbed him and held him in place for a long kiss. He found himself responding soon and earned himself another A plus from the schoolmarm.

17

Slocum hitched up his gun belt and marched into the court-house. He had spent a delightful night with Angela and felt like he could whip his weight in polecats. The judge's clerk came from a side room and started to speak. Morris saw how determined Slocum was and clamped his mouth shut before taking a step back into his cramped office.

Rapping once on the judge's door, Slocum did not wait for an answer. He opened the door to see a surprised Judge Tunstell. The man reached for the pistol in his shoulder rig, but then relaxed when he recognized Slocum.

"You in the habit of barging into a judge's office, Mr. Slocum?" Tunstell asked.

"I am today. I have too many questions that need answers." Slocum saw how Tunstell tensed at this. He knew what was coming and did not cotton much to it.

"Close the door," Tunstell said.

Slocum already had. He dropped into the chair and stared at the judge for what seemed an eternity. This sometimes worked in poker games. Slocum could stare down his opponent until mistakes were made that Slocum could capitalize on. The judge was too savvy for that.

"The mayor's killed a couple men," Slocum finally said.

"With Marshal Delgado laid up, what are you going to do about it?"

"You have proof?"

"You know as well as I do who robbed the stagecoach and who stole your precious legal papers. Why did Grierson want to stop you from throwing Bennigan off his claim?"

"Who says he robbed the stage? Or is guilty of any of the other things you say?"

"I recognized him in spite of his mask. I trailed him the best I could on foot right after the robbery. His horse had a loose shoe, which the farrier was fixing when I got to town. Later on, he had the box stolen from him."

"Indeed? By the robber responsible for the shoot-out that killed Mr. Kinney?"

"I've been thinking on that, Judge," Slocum said. "All the lead came from inside the bank. One robber was already dead and the other two were outside the bank getting onto their horses. Could be that Williams cut down Kinney. He was flinging lead around in a mighty wild fashion."

Slocum knew he had hit a bull's-eye. Tunstell turned pale and averted his eyes guiltily.

"There's a whole lot more I could lay out for you. Mostly, though, I want to know why you want Bennigan off his claim. I've been in that mine. It's nigh on worthless. And why would you care, even if he had hit the mother lode? You and your partners have an entire town to milk."

"I take exception with that, Mr. Slocum."

"Don't doubt it, but it's still true. What's Bennigan got that you don't?"

Tunstell got to his feet and began to pace. His highly polished shoes made no sound as they crushed into his deep-pile Oriental carpet. Pacing with his hands locked behind his back, head down, Tunstell finally came to a halt at his window. He stared out at the town. His shoulders rose and fell as if he vented a deep, heartfelt sigh.

"It should not have come unraveled like this, but Grierson is getting greedy."

"Not Williams, too?"

Tunstell shrugged but did not turn to look at Slocum.

"I did not choose my business associates well, it seems," the judge said. "The bank robbery was a farce. Grierson and I both know it. Williams took our money—"

"From the Mojave East Farming Company?"

This revelation caused Tunstell to spin. His hand went for his pistol again. He relaxed when he realized killing Slocum would do nothing to stem the flow of information he had once counted on as being secret.

"You snoop too much, Mr. Slocum."

"I do what I can. It's mighty hard not asking around."

"Nobody in town knows that name. Well, my clerk does. But he's such a pusillanimous pup he would piss his pants even thinking about revealing what he knows."

"You haven't been able to get your money back from Williams?"

"Grierson has suggested some rather dire methods, but I have held back. I'm not sure I want to much longer," Tunstell said. "All I wanted was to have a grove of fruit trees. Peach, apple, cherry. I love cherry trees. Good fruit, excellent wood. It could have happened, too."

"Trees require . . . water," Slocum said, his voice trailing off as things fell into place. "Bennigan's mine is flooded. He's tapped into an underground river and you want the water for irrigation."

"Succinctly put, Mr. Slocum. I want this entire valley to bloom. It can, with sufficient water."

"You want to own it all."

"Of course. I make no bones about that. I thought Grierson and Williams shared my dreams."

"Dreams of avarice grow faster than a man can lasso," Slocum said.

"So it seems, at least with Williams. He has our money. He has our money and no vision. Irrigation in this region with its rich land could return a thousand times that much in a few years. He is content with a few paltry thousand."

"He probably gunned down Delgado, too. I think the marshal figured out what was going on."

"A killer and a coward." Tunstell laughed without humor. "That's the Dry Water banker."

"Grierson killed Marcus Ross, too."

"Who?"

"The robber in the jailhouse. He did it to cover up Williams's theft of the money."

"They were in it together? They teamed up against me? I would not have thought they were good enough friends for that."

"They might hate each other's guts, but as you said, the immediate lure of money is powerful for men without vision."

"So why are they still in town?"

"I don't think Grierson knows where Williams hid the money. He might, but it's more likely he's keeping Williams alive to find out what happened to the money."

"Buried somewhere near town," Tunstell said.

"Grierson also has the papers evicting Bennigan that you wanted signed up in Sacramento. Why would he stop that?"

"He might think to deal me out entirely. Or maybe Williams is the one with the dreams of growing and Grierson wants to use those papers to lure him. Who can say what schemes are spun between them. Mine was simple. Get Bennigan's water. The Mojave East already owns all the surrounding land."

"I know," Slocum said.

"If you know about the Mojave East, you must know it all," Tunstell agreed. "What do you intend to do, Mr. Slocum? You have smoked me out."

"Can't say that you've done anything criminal. Trying to throw Cal Bennigan off his claim isn't right, but it might be legal."

"Oh, yes, it is all legal," Tunstell said. "He might have made a decent manager for my farm, too."

"I doubt it," Slocum said. He had seen too many hard-rock miners in his day. Nothing mattered to those solitary souls but scrabbling in the cold, dark, underground tunnels for the merest flake of gold.

"What are you going to do, Mr. Slocum? My destiny is in your hands."

"I doubt that, Judge," Slocum said. "But what I'm going to do? That's easy enough. I spent the night thinking on it. Let me tell you what I've got in mind."

Judge Tunstell perked up as Slocum began laying out his plan.

Slocum pulled his hat down a little farther and tried to look inconspicuous. He leaned back against the building as the mayor hurried past him. Slocum let out his pent-up breath because Grierson never even glanced in his direction. But Angela Ross did. She ran along after the mayor. She shot Slocum a broad smile and gave him a wink. Then she was around the corner out of his sight.

"Mr. Mayor, please, wait a moment. Please, sir, please. I must talk to you. It is urgent."

Slocum sidled closer to the corner of the building and found a decent spot to crouch and eavesdrop. Angela had stopped Grierson not two paces down the boardwalk.

"Miss Enwright. What can I do for you?"

"I don't know what to do with the marshal still laid up the way he is. I went to see him just now but he was sleeping. Drugs or something. He is in such great pain when he is not sleeping."

"I'm aware of Marshal Delgado's condition, Miss Enwright," Grierson said. "If you'll excuse me, I have a meeting."

"Who do I report that awful robber to?"

Slocum almost laughed. He imagined the expression on Grierson's face. The mayor was about to take a step and almost fell when he broke his stride.

"The one who robbed the bank?"

"That's the problem, Mayor Grierson," Angela said in a worried tone. "He was with Mr. Williams."

"What?"

"They were divvying up a stack of money. It might not have been much but it looked like a great deal to me. Why, it was more than six inches high, all piled-up greenbacks."

"Where? Where did you see this?"

"Out back of the schoolhouse," she said. "Not more than an hour ago. I had to dismiss the children, of course, then I went to the marshal and—"

"They were splitting the money?"

"Between themselves. The robber wore that same shirt. The blue and white one. I'd say he has plenty of money to buy a new one now."

"Williams and the robber?"

"They were quite friendly. I thought nothing of it until they began counting the money, and I remembered that the robber wore such a shirt. It was hard to miss that, believe me. I wish I got a fraction of that much money to buy books for the children."

"How long ago did you say?"

"Almost an hour," Angela said. "What should I do, Mayor Grierson?"

"You've done the right thing, my dear. Telling me is all you have to do to rest easy. Run along and forget all about this now."

"Well, I have done the right thing telling you, I suppose."

"You have, you have."

Slocum heard the anxiety in the mayor's tone. He didn't bother repressing a smile at Angela. She turned a little and looked at him, licked her lips just a little and then shook her bustle even more in wanton invitation. Slocum would have liked to get under that bustle but there was no time. The sharp click of the mayor's boots on the boardwalk went in the other direction. Fast.

Slocum got to his feet and ran to the rear of the building where Conchita stood patiently. He swung into the saddle and walked his horse toward the schoolhouse. To his surprise, the mayor was nowhere to be seen. Putting his spurs to Conchita's flanks, he galloped to the livery stable.

He yelled to the stableman, "Has Grierson just left?"

"Well, yeah, Slocum, he has. He went that way." The man pointed out of town.

Slocum pulled down his hat and galloped hard. He slowed only when he felt Conchita begin to tire. Looking all around, he saw no sign of the mayor. Slocum cursed under his breath. He had guessed wrong what was going on. Williams might have stolen the money, but Grierson knew where it was and headed directly there. Slowing his breakneck pace to a walk brought a snort of thanks from Conchita, but Slocum had to work along the road carefully if he wanted to find where Grierson had ridden.

The mayor had gone only a mile out of town before cutting from the road and heading into a patch of desert that would kill any man caught out here without sufficient water. The hard-baked ground did not take hoofprints easily, but Slocum was close enough behind that the occasional sandy patches still showed tracks he could follow. Even as he rode, he felt a hot wind at his back blowing off the Mojave. That wind would evaporate his sweat and keep him cool. It would also erase Grierson's tracks.

Slocum rode faster, guessing at the trail now. The area turned into rolling dunes. Once he risked riding to the top to look over. If Grierson happened to be watching his back trail, he would have spotted Slocum instantly.

Instead, Slocum caught sight of the deliberately riding mayor. The man had his head down and kept his horse trotting along at a brisk enough pace to wear it out within a few miles.

Slocum dismounted and watched, giving Conchita a little rest while he figured where Grierson went. The desert gave way to some rocky terrain. Grierson made a beeline for it. Slocum decided what would be his best route to approach unobserved. Grierson came in directly from the east. Curving around and approaching from the northeast would shield Slocum from immediate discovery.

He fingered the ebony butt of his six-shooter and then mounted. It was time to recover some money.

Turning cautious after he had circled and had come up on Grierson, Slocum finally dropped to the sand and found a low-growing creosote bush on which to tether Conchita. From here he advanced on foot. Using the rise of a dune to hide himself, he got to the top and flopped down to see Grierson in the middle of a large bowl of hard-packed sand. The man walked this way and that, seemingly at random, until Slocum guessed he was pacing off directions. Grierson dropped to his knees in the midst of the sand and ran his hands over the ground.

Slocum heard the man's screech of anger all the way up to the top of the dune.

Grierson started digging like a dog hunting for a bone, sending sand flying. In a few minutes, he stopped and rested on all fours, like a dog panting from the heat. Grierson pushed to his feet, spat into the hole he had dug, turned and left empty-handed.

"So," Slocum mused. "The crook has been robbed." Knowing he had his work cut out for him, Slocum slid back down the far side of the dune and returned to his horse. He got back to Dry Water only minutes after Grierson.

All hell was breaking loose.

18

"I saw him riding into town a while back. Never saw him that mad before," Judge Tunstell told Slocum. "What got his tail in a wringer?"

"Williams stole the money from the bank," Slocum said, "and the mayor must have stolen it from him."

"Son of a bitch," muttered Tunstell. Slocum was not sure if the judge meant the men or simply swore as a matter of course while taking in the whole wretched situation.

"Where'd he go?"

"Kept on riding," Tunstell said. "He glanced into the bank, never dismounted, then lit out like all the demons of hell were after him."

"Nothing chasing him," Slocum said. "He's after Williams. Unless he gets the money back right away, he's likely to kill Williams, too."

"No loss if he ventilates that skunk," the judge said, "but I'd like to get my money back. A third of it belongs to me."

Slocum heard a touch of hope in the judge's voice. Tunstell hoped for more than getting the money he put into the Mojave East Company. He wanted it all.

"Where does Williams live?" He studied the brick bank building and wondered what was on the second floor. It might hold the banker's quarters, but if Grierson rode out of town, he knew where to find his partner.

His former partner, Slocum corrected himself.

"I'll show you."

"I can—"

Slocum cut off his protest when he saw the way Tunstell glared at him. In his day, the judge must have been a capable man with a gun. The pistol in his shoulder rig came to hand so fast Slocum wondered if he would ever want to face him.

"I was a sheriff before I became a lawyer and a judge," Tunstell told him. "I brought in the Panhandle Kid and his partner, Big Ears Johnson."

Slocum had never heard of them, but the judge spoke with such intensity that the arrest must have forged part of his life that turned him to law and away from crime. Still, the judge walked a narrow road with what he tried to do to Cal Bennigan to get the man's water.

"That's not going to be necessary," Slocum said. "If Williams doesn't cut down Grierson, then Grierson will kill the banker."

"I'd rather see them both swing for what they've done. That'd make it all legal," Tunstell said.

"They go to trial, there's no keeping them from telling about your part in the scheme to do Bennigan out of his claim. They might try to tar you with the same brush—the one that'll see them both convicted of murder."

For a moment Tunstell said nothing. Then he squared his shoulders.

"I am an officer of the court and will uphold the law to the best of my ability. I want them both tried."

"You're a dangerous man," Slocum said. "An honest judge." He saw that the law meant more to Tunstell than his own neck. He should have realized this earlier when Tunstell insisted on evicting Bennigan legally from his mine. It was all legal hocus-pocus but it would have been done by the law and not the six-shooter, the way Williams had wanted it.

"You wait here, Slocum. It won't take me a minute to fetch my horse."

Slocum chafed at the delay but knew better than to go hunting for Grierson and Williams on his own. Tunstell knew where to find them. The judge rode around the courthouse and pointed down the main street like a general ordering a frontal assault on enemy lines.

Slocum kicked at Conchita to get up to a matching speed. They galloped through town and out, attracting some attention. A small town like Dry Water had little in the way of entertainment save for gossip. Slocum knew the new schoolmarm would have triggered a passel of loose talk, but seeing the judge and Slocum riding after the mayor had to keep the townsfolk busy for hours cussing and discussing the situation.

"What part does that young filly have in all this, Mr. Slocum?"

Slocum looked over at the judge. The man rode well, but he turned slightly toward Slocum as if he might be hard of hearing.

"How do you mean?"

"The dead outlaw was named Marcus Ross. I am positive the Angela Enwright who answered my ad was supposed to be much older. Our Miss Enwright's real name wouldn't happen to be Ross, also, would it? Husband and wife?"

"Brother and sister," Slocum said.

"That's good," Tunstell said. "For you and her. It never pays to commit adultery. In some ways, that's worse than stealing a man's horse. What of the other bank robber? Also a relative?"

"Her other brother."

"A useful combination. She gets a job teaching school, the children tell her all manner of useful things about banks and stagecoaches and how money flows through a town. There's no limit to what urchins notice about their elders' business, and they never realize it. So she finds when to rob the town, and her brothers perform the dirty deed." Tunstell looked hard at Slocum. "Does she take the loot and hide it so that if they are caught they can deny involvement?"

"Don't rightly know that, Judge," Slocum said. "She did hide her brother after he shot out the mayor's window."

"I wondered about that. Grierson is a clever one. He knew you were leading the posse on a wild-goose chase. Where was Miss Ross's brother?"

Slocum hesitated, then said, "Under the floorboards in the classroom."

Tunstell laughed. "That might be the best use that old schoolhouse has been put to in years. Lord knows the children aren't learning a speck of what they need to know."

Slocum considered that as they rode along the road, turning toward a whitewashed house some distance off the road and sitting atop a hill. How good a teacher was Angela? He grinned ruefully and knew it hardly mattered. She had taught him enough and maybe he had taught her a thing or two that didn't show up in textbooks. His mind wandered over to how different the robbery might have been had Angela come to town, scouted out the bank and Roger Williams, then had her three brothers commit the robbery.

Roger Williams might well have had ten thousand dollars stashed in the bank and it would have been taken by the Ross gang.

"There's Grierson," Tunstell said. "We shouldn't disturb him just yet."

"I'll scout."

"So will I," the judge said. Their eyes locked. Slocum knew there was no way to argue with him. He pointed to a gully where they could hide their horses. They trotted down and found shelter for their animals. Conchita nickered softly and looked at Slocum with big brown eyes, as if accusing him of pushing her too far, too hard that day. He patted the horse's neck and then dismounted.

To his surprise, Tunstell was already making his way up toward the house, moving silently. Slocum followed, noting how the judge moved. He had seen Indians unable to move so quietly and swiftly. They came to a spot just under a window in the large house. From this vantage Williams had a good view of anyone coming to visit, except from the direction the judge had come. Again Tunstell's skill impressed Slocum.

"Can you see anything?" Tunstell was too short to see into the high window. Slocum chanced a quick peek.

"Both of them are inside. I can't hear what they're saying, but they are arguing."

"Come on around back. There's a door we might be able to open so we can eavesdrop better." Tunstell moved with more speed now and created something of a ruckus when he knocked over a pail. The two men froze, hands on their six-shooters, but Grierson and Williams were too engrossed in their argument to notice.

Tunstell opened the door a few inches and peered in. Slocum stood on the other side of the door, back against the wall, and listened hard. He could make out what the banker and mayor said if he remained still.

"You stole it!" Williams cried. "I had it all hid and you stole it!"

"You wanted to cut me out of my share, you miserable bastard," Grierson said. "Where'd you move it?"

"I saw how you dug up the money when I hid it right after the robbery."

"You stole our money, Williams. That was the only robbery."

"Those three were so clumsy I had to take the money. Let them take the blame."

"You shot the one in the back," Grierson accused.

"You gunned down the other in his jail cell! Who's the murderer, Grierson? Me shooting at a robber getting away, or you shooting an unarmed man like he was a duck swimming in a water barrel!"

Slocum and Tunstell exchanged glances. The men inside continued to accuse each other of the worst possible crimes. Tunstell tightened his grip on his pistol. Slocum motioned for him to stay put. The men had confessed to all manner of crimes, but Slocum wanted more. He wanted the money Williams had spirited away from the bank.

"I had to protect it," Grierson said. "You hid it where any fool could stumble over it."

"I didn't have much time. I had to act fast. And what do you mean you had to protect the money? From me? I was lucky to see you digging it up. I trailed you out into the desert. You hadn't even tamped down the dirt and had barely ridden off when I had the money back."

"You may have the money but I've got Tunstell's papers."

"Who cares about Bennigan and his water? I never wanted to grow crops. I prefer greenbacks and gold dust, thank you," said Williams.

"That's the banker in you talking. With the money and the water, we can become the biggest farmers in the whole damn state."

"Grierson, you don't know the first damn thing about farming. You're as big a crook as I am. Bigger. You've killed a prisoner locked up in a cell."

Slocum had to reach out and push Tunstell back. The best was about to come. He felt it.

"We got to work together," Grierson said. "This whole house of cards is falling down around us."

"You only want to know where I hid the money."

"We can trust each other."

"Cut the judge out?" suggested Williams.

"I have the papers he said only he could file. He was lying. All I need to do is change his name to ours, and we can take Bennigan's water. You have the money. Together, we can own this whole damn town. Think how much we can make off it."

"I am, Grierson, I am," said the banker. "All right. I'll show you where I hid the money."

Tunstell started to go in, gun blazing, and again Slocum cautioned him to stay out of sight.

"Let them get the money," Slocum whispered. "That'll go a ways toward clearing Hank Ross of the crime."

"I don't care about him," growled Tunstell. "Those two—" Tunstell began sputtering uncharacteristically.

"We'll trail them and catch them red-handed with the money. Will that satisfy you? Put their necks in a noose, if you like. You'll get your money back. Maybe those legal papers, too."

"The ones you lost," snapped Tunstell.

"The ones Grierson stole. I wasn't going to take a bullet for a packet of papers. I didn't know then that was what he wanted, either."

"Sorry, Slocum." Tunstell swung the door open a few more inches and stuck his head inside. "They're gone. You reckon Williams might have hidden the loot here?"

"He might be taking Grierson on a snipe hunt, but I don't think so. Grierson would kill him outright."

The sound of horses leaving spurred Slocum and Tunstell to circle the house, going in opposite directions. Slocum waved to the judge when he got to the front. Grierson and Williams had ridden back down the road, making no attempt to hurry.

Slocum and Tunstell retrieved their horses and followed at a safe distance. Worrying that Grierson might get edgy and spot them, Slocum urged the judge to hang back even farther than necessary.

"They won't notice any dust we might kick up," the judge protested. "I want to keep them both in sight." He grunted and added, "In my sights." His right hand clenched, as if he still held his six-gun and his finger was curled around the trigger.

"Tracking them isn't going to be too hard. I don't think Williams would have gone far to hide the money."

"You're right. He stole it back from Grierson. He would want it where he could keep an eye on it."

"Up there," Slocum said, pointing to a hill opposite Williams's house. "He could sit on his front porch and watch it night and day, if he wanted."

"Those rocks would be a perfect spot to stash the money,"

Tunstell agreed. "They'll be able to see us, if that's where they're heading."

"Not if we cut across country right now," Slocum said. Conchita found a game trail that took them away from the summit of the low hill. Tunstell protested, but Slocum trusted the sturdy pony. The trail circled around and then worked up the backside of the hill.

"I need to place more confidence in you and your abilities, Mr. Slocum," the judge said. "Or is it only the marshal's pony?"

"It's all Conchita's doing," Slocum said, looking at the horse. She might look like a swaybacked nag but the horse had heart and more intelligence than any dozen horses Slocum had seen.

"I see them. About where you thought."

The words were hardly out of Tunstell's mouth when a single gunshot rang out. They both lashed their horses to more speed, getting up the hill. They found themselves on the summit but on the far side of huge rocks. Scrambling, pistols drawn, they made their way around the rock in time to see Williams riding away as if his tail were on fire. Sprawled on the rocky ground lay Grierson. His sightless eyes stared up at the bright California sky.

"Buzzard bait," Tunstell grumbled. "And I wanted to stretch his neck."

Slocum kicked at some rocks that had been moved recently. There might have been something hidden in the cranny but he couldn't tell. All he saw were bright scratches on the rocks that had been moved, as if something metallic had been dragged along their surface. "Looks like Williams was in a mighty big hurry. Don't see any of the loot, though."

"He's not going back to Dry Water. He's hightailing it," Tunstell said. The judge stared at Slocum. "You up to being deputized and bringing him to justice?"

"Forget the deputy's badge and having the town pay me," Slocum said. "I'll do this one for nothing." He kicked Grierson in the ribs, just to make sure. The body rolled slightly but otherwise Slocum saw no movement. Already voracious black flies were landing on the mayor's face.

Slocum slid his Colt Navy back into its holster and went to the horses. To his surprise, Tunstell was only a few paces behind.

"I want to be in on this, Slocum. I thought maybe I ought to stay with Grierson. But what's the point? He's already got enough friends to look after him."

"Flies, coyotes, buzzards," Slocum said. "Too good for a man who guns down another man locked up in a jail cell."

"My sentiments, too," Tunstell said. "Think we'll have a hard chase?"

"Doubt it," Slocum said. He swung his horse around. Conchita tried to buck, but he held her down and got the horse to follow the game trail back down around the knob of rocks atop the hill. Finding where Williams had ridden was simple. The man was galloping like a fool and would tire his horse out within a couple miles.

"On this terrain, it won't be more than a mile," Tunstell said, as if reading Slocum's thoughts. The judge grinned. "I used to be a fair tracker, myself. And I know horses." He patted the big black horse he rode. As powerful as the stallion was, Tunstell might be able to outride Williams by miles and miles. He was content to keep to the pace set by Conchita.

They moved at a steady clip but found that Williams had angled for the hills to the east of town. That made tracking both harder and easier. The rocky ground didn't take hoofprints, but the number of places where the renegade banker might head was limited. Slocum had picked out a notch in the hills. He had no idea what lay on the far side of that pass, but Williams went for it straight as an arrow.

"Goes into the desert," Tunstell said. "He's a damn fool thinking he can get away going there."

"Tell me something I haven't figured out for myself," Slocum said. He tugged on his reins to stop Conchita. Something didn't seem right to him. Slocum dropped to the ground and studied the ground, scowled and began a wide circle.

"What's wrong, Mr. Slocum?"

"Don't know, but something is. Williams slowed here. To a walk. And stopped. I see where his horse broke a few of those low branches on a bush."

"And?"

"He didn't keep on the trail for the pass. He cut away and is riding along the hills. What's in that direction?"

"Nothing. He'd have to turn back if he wanted to go to Dry Water."

"He's not going to do that. Williams wants nothing more than to avoid everyone in town," Slocum said. He pushed back his hat and wiped at the sweat on his forehead as he tried to figure out what Williams was up to. "Might be he has a hideout in the hills."

"Williams? I doubt he would think that far ahead. Everything he's done has been on the spur of the moment," Tunstell said. "He probably wasn't looking to steal the Mojave East money until the robbery, then saw his chance and took it. Grierson was the schemer. Williams reacts."

"If that's so, he reacted to something in that direction." Slocum looked in the direction opposite to the way Williams had ridden. On foot he scouted the area but found nothing. "Something must have spooked him real bad but I can't figure what changed his mind about going across the pass," Slocum finally admitted.

As he went to mount, he stopped and pulled a small piece of cloth off a thornbush. He ran it between his fingers, then looked at it more closely.

"Find something?"

"Reckon not," Slocum said, tucking the scrap into his pocket and turning away.

He swung into the saddle and set off after Williams again. He had ridden less than a quarter mile when he put his finger to his lips and then pointed to his left. A horse snorted and pawed at the sandy bottom of an arroyo.

"Williams's horse," the judge said. "I don't see him, though."

"I do," said Slocum. He jumped from his horse and drew his six-shooter. It wasn't needed.

He went to the banker, lying near the bank of the arroyo. Williams moaned and stirred but could not rise.

"Looks like he got thrown and hit his head on a rock," Tunstell said.

Slocum didn't dispute the matter, but that wasn't the way it looked to him.

"Wha—where am I?"

"You're in custody, you poisonous sidewinder," Tunstell said. "I'm hauling your sorry ass back to Dry Water so you can stand trial."

Slocum waited for the judge to figure out the obvious. It took him only a few more seconds.

"Where's the money?"

Slocum looked around but could not find it. The judge looked even harder and failed to turn up even a single green-back.

"Where'd you hide the money?" Tunstell demanded.

Williams rubbed the back of his head and moaned.

"I don't know. I was slugged. Somebody must have taken the money."

"You took the money, you lying sack of shit," Tunstell raged. "Where did you hide it?"

Williams shook his head and moaned some more. His denials rang hollow all the way back to the Dry Water jail.

19

"You certain you're up to the task, Marshal?" Slocum looked at Delgado, propped up behind his desk with a couple pillows to support his back and neck. He was almost as white as the linen pillowcases, and his hands shook when he reached out to brace himself against the desk.

"I'm right as rain, Slocum. Don't worry. I'm not letting that one get out of my jailhouse." Delgado jerked his thumb over his shoulder in the direction of the cell where Roger Williams was safely locked. "That *pendejo* was the one who shot me. I happened in just as the robbery was winding down. When I turned to go after the robber, Williams shot me. Three times." Delgado winced as he moved. "The only way he's getting out of my jailhouse is when he's headed for the gallows."

"Looks to happen soon enough," Slocum said. "The judge wanted to try him right away but couldn't find anyone willing to defend him. There's a lawyer coming from Sacramento in a few days."

"Don't matter to me if it's a few months," Delgado declared. "Williams isn't going to escape justice this time." The marshal grinned and it wasn't pleasant. "Fact is, the longer he's in my custody, the sooner he'll want to have a noose dropped around his neck."

"You watch out," Slocum cautioned. "He's as slippery as a greased pig."

"Go on, Slocum. The judge wanted to see you pronto."

Slocum nodded to the marshal, stepped out into the hot desert sun and took a deep breath of the searing air. It felt good being on this side of the iron bars. It was something Williams would never again experience. With a confident stride, Slocum marched over to the courthouse and to the judge's door. He started to barge in, then politely knocked and waited for Tunstell to ask him in.

"Wondered why it was taking you so long to get here, Mr. Slocum," the judge said. "You've been over at the jail seeing how our marshal is getting on."

"Is that a guess or did someone tell you?"

"You caught me. My clerk told me. He saw you heading in that direction. Morris is trying to curry favor with me and tries not to miss anything going on in town that might interest me. Unfortunately, most of what he tells me is of no interest at all."

"Williams is safely locked up. The marshal is weak but alert. He won't let another prisoner get out of his jail unless it's to go to the gallows. But I reckon Morris has already told you all that."

The sound of hammering made Slocum look up. Out the window of the judge's office he saw the freshly sawed wooden-plank gallows being built not fifty yards away. "Isn't that premature? He hasn't stood trial yet."

"I have a sense that justice will be served," Tunstell said. He rocked back in his chair and tented his fingers so he could rest his chin on the tips. "I've been thinking about the whole sorry mess."

Slocum sank into the chair opposite the desk and waited. He knew what was going to come and was ready for it.

"What happened to the money from the bank? There might not have been ten thousand as Williams claimed, but the entire working capital of the Mojave East Company was there. My accounts say it was close to six thousand dollars."

"Do tell," Slocum said. "The way I see it, Williams led Grierson to an empty hole. They argued and Williams got the drop on Grierson."

"That doesn't say anything about where the money is. Williams stole it—back—from Grierson. Grierson had hidden it in the desert, Williams recovered it and where did he put it?"

"Do you need all that money, Judge? The Mojave East Company is pretty much dead now, I would say."

"I hate to lose the money and any chance of getting Bennigan's property, signed, sealed and delivered to my pocket."

"Been thinking on that. Do you need to *own* his property or just the water rights?"

"What do I care about the other mineral rights? There's no gold there."

"Bennigan thinks so," Slocum said.

Tunstell looked at him sharply.

"What do you have up your sleeve, Mr. Slocum?"

"Would you be willing to help Calvin Bennigan pump the water from his mine in return for cancellation of all liens and back taxes and attempts to take his property?"

"You mean pump out the water I want and let him keep a worthless hole in the ground?"

"That's about right, Judge."

"Damn, but that is a simple solution. Why didn't I see it before?"

"Because you're a lawyer," Slocum said, pulling a crumpled piece of paper from his coat pocket. He handed it to the judge. "It's not all prettified in legal words, but it says what I just told you."

"Not too badly done. Hmm, the water's got to be pumped out at my expense. I'm not sure—"

"Take it or leave it. I told Bennigan you would be inclined to help him drain the two lowest levels of his mine. There's a powerful lot of water there. Not brackish." He ran his hand over his lips. He remembered the dirt taste of that water. It had never occurred to him that it could be used for something other than drinking. An orchard would not care if the water tasted good, as long as it wasn't salty. Crops of all kinds could flourish in dirty water.

"I should give up my judgeship and put you on the bench, Mr. Slocum. You're a clever man."

Tunstell read the contract again, nodding to himself. Slocum waited until the judge satisfied himself all was as outlined.

"I'll sign it." He took his pen out, dipped it in the well and put his signature on the bottom of the page with a flourish. "We'll get all this recorded."

"And you will be able to start your orchard before the fall. That's why you were in such a hurry, wasn't it? You wanted to get the trees in before cold weather."

"It gets mighty frigid in the desert during the winter. I have to let the trees take root for at least three months. More's better."

"Horses, orchards, you the sole political power in Dry Water. You have come out on top, Judge."

"So it seems, Mr. Slocum, thanks to you." Tunstell studied Slocum for a moment, then asked, "When are you moving on?"

"Right away." Slocum appreciated that Judge Tunstell did not try to make an offer to hold him in Dry Water. There was nothing, even the promise of being foreman on a fine stud ranch, to hold him this close to the edge of the desert. He had been hankering for a view of the ocean and now he could satisfy that yen.

"I do wonder about the money Williams stole," Tunstell said, his eyes fixed hard on Slocum.

"The way I see it, Judge, Williams was double-crossing Grierson again. He took him to a spot where he might have hidden the money but hadn't. Grierson got to looking, Williams got the drop on him and cut him down. Saves the town the cost of a second trial and noose." Slocum looked outside to where the gallows was completely erected now. Two men worked with sandbags and ropes to get the proper length of drop and weight for the condemned's satisfactory execution.

"An empty hole in the ground. Hardly seems right."

"Get Williams to confess where he really hid the money," Slocum said. "Tell him confession might save his soul."

"He's a banker. He has no soul."

"Some might say that about lawyers," Slocum said, his gaze as hard as the judge's.

"Yes, they might. But not in Dry Water. Hope you find what you are looking for, Mr. Slocum. Wherever it might be."

Slocum stood, shook hands with the judge and then went outside. He had dickered a little with Marshal Delgado over Conchita. The marshal had finally given the horse to him. Slocum gave the horse a lump of sugar, mounted and then rode out of town. When he came to the fork in the road, the well traveled one going west to Pemberton and the lesser route into the hills, he turned east.

The hills appeared deceptively close, but Conchita was a steady mount and Slocum reached the distant hills about sundown. He knew the trail well, having taken it several times before through the pass and into the valley beyond. The Ross gang had made their camp here.

He saw the slight curl of smoke rising and caught the mouthwatering scent of roasting venison. Hank Ross was one fine cook.

Slocum rode into the camp. Ross worked to turn the haunch of meat on a green stick spit. He looked up.

"Wondered if we would see you today, Slocum," he said.

"Am I in time for dinner?"

"Pull up a rock."

"I found some wild roots that taste a little like potatoes, too," Angela said, coming up holding her skirt so she could carry some of the dirty tubers.

Slocum settled down and watched as the two went about their preparation.

"You ought to open a restaurant," Slocum said.

"Hank was the cook on a cattle drive. That's where he learned to make just about any hunk of dried leather into a decent meal. He's a far better cook than I am."

"Angel's not too bad, either. Ma doted on her."

They ate, chatting about small things.

When they finished, Slocum said, "How much money had Williams made off with?"

"We've divvied it up already, John." Angela fumbled in a bedroll and pulled out a metal box. Slocum remembered the bright scratches on the sides of the rocks where Williams had taken Grierson. The box had made those scratches when Williams had pulled it free from its hiding place.

"So?" Slocum watched the two closely.

"Thirty-one hundred dollars each," she said.

"Exactly?"

Angela laughed. "You can trust my arithmetic. I am a schoolmarm, after all." She turned it around so the lid hid the contents as she opened the box. Slocum tensed. Then he relaxed. She took out three bundles tied up pretty-like with ribbon, handing one to her brother, keeping one and handing the third to Slocum.

Slocum tucked the wad of greenbacks into his pocket.

"You aren't going to count it?" Hank Ross's eyebrows arched.

"Why should I?" asked Slocum. "I trust my partners."

He looked from Hank to Angela. Her bright eyes danced with joy.

"And we trust ours," she said.

The three of them rode out the next morning, heading for Tucson. Somehow, Slocum didn't mind that much missing out on seeing the Pacific Ocean.

Watch for

SLOCUM AND THE BIG HORN TRAIL

349th novel in the exciting SLOCUM series
from Jove

Coming in March!

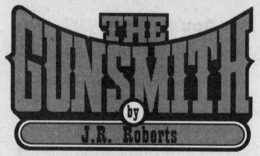

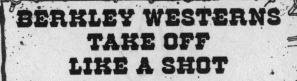